Donut
Goals

Donut
Goals

Coco Simon

Simon Spotlight

New York   London   Toronto   Sydney   New Delhi

This book is a work of fiction. Any references to historical events, real people, or real places are used fictitiously. Other names, characters, places, and events are products of the author's imagination, and any resemblance to actual events or places or persons, living or dead, is entirely coincidental.

SIMON SPOTLIGHT
An imprint of Simon & Schuster Children's Publishing Division
1230 Avenue of the Americas, New York, New York 10020
This Simon Spotlight paperback edition August 2021
Copyright © 2021 by Simon & Schuster, Inc.
All rights reserved, including the right of reproduction in whole or in part in any form.
SIMON SPOTLIGHT and colophon are registered trademarks of Simon & Schuster, Inc.
Text by Mary Tillworth
For information about special discounts for bulk purchases, please contact
Simon & Schuster Special Sales at 1-866-506-1949 or business@simonandschuster.com.
Designed by Ciara Gay
The text of this book was set in Bembo Std.
Manufactured in the United States of America 0721 OFF
10 9 8 7 6 5 4 3 2 1
ISBN 978-1-5344-9598-2 (hc)
ISBN 978-1-5344-9597-5 (pbk)
ISBN 978-1-5344-9599-9 (ebook)
Library of Congress Catalog Card Number 2021940291

Chapter One

Running Is the Best Thing

Riiiiing!!!

I jumped out of my seat and grabbed my backpack, which was hanging from my chair. School was finally out!

Hoisting my backpack across my shoulders, I ran out the door and hurried to my locker. Even though I like my classes and can sit still and pay attention during them, my legs are always itching to leave by the end of the day.

I know that I left recess behind in elementary school, but there's part of me that really wishes that I could have brought it with me into middle school.

I love the idea of being able to go out into the sunshine after a few hours of classes and stretch and run. I would ignore the tetherballs and basketball hoops and make a beeline for the group of kids playing tag.

In the short time we had outside, I'd run and duck and swerve, sometimes getting close to the tagger, then spinning around and flying toward the "safe" wall of the school building. I loved the feeling of excitement of outrunning somebody, or dodging their outstretched hand as I bolted across the playground.

But now, in sixth grade, recess is gone. Sure, I've got gym class scheduled, but even though I have gym two to three times a week, it still never feels like enough exercise.

I am lucky, though—there is one sport that I've been playing for six years that helps me feel happy in my body. Mom and Dad signed me up for soccer when I was in kindergarten, and I've been playing ever since.

I love the way it feels when I'm totally concentrated on the ball, dribbling and passing and moving it forward to the opposing team's goal. Even though my body is working hard, it's a special moment when my head gets really quiet as it focuses on the next play.

Run, dribble, pass, repeat, score!

I had soccer practice the next day, but today I was walking home with my sister Kelsey. I found her by the front of the school, and together we started on our way.

Kelsey and I are really close in age, but we don't share a lot of things in common.

For one thing, Mom and Dad are Kelsey's birth mother and father, while I was adopted by them from South Korea when I was just a baby.

Kelsey looks like a combination of my parents, with her light brown hair and green eyes, while I've got straight black hair and dark brown eyes.

My sister is super disorganized, while I like to keep track of all my things. (Don't look in my closet, though—it is the one part of my life that I allow to go a little haywire.) Kelsey also isn't always on time, while I hate it when I'm even a minute late for things.

But despite our differences, I love having Kelsey as a sister. And I feel protective of her too.

A while back, when her personal blog accidentally got posted to the web, even though there wasn't anything really sensitive that she shared, I made a plan to get her out of school that day and home with Mom and Dad so she didn't have to be around the kids who had just read her innermost thoughts. I think that helping her drew the two of us closer together.

"Want to go for a run when we get home?" I asked Kelsey as we walked along.

I held my finger in the air as if I was testing it. The air was sharp and crisp, cool, but not the kind of cool that makes you want to stay inside.

"It's the perfect weather for it."

Kelsey shook her head. "Nah. I'm reading a really good book, and I'm almost done with it. I want to see what happens in the end."

She shrugged, adjusting her backpack. "Plus, I feel like I haven't been paying enough attention to Rusty lately. I kind of feel like snuggle time is on the horizon."

I nodded. Rusty is the dog we adopted recently. One of our neighbors, Mrs. Rose, helps out at a local rescue shelter, fostering dogs until they're adopted so they don't have to be kept in the shelter's kennels all the time.

One day Mrs. Rose was walking by my soccer practice with a couple of dogs that she was fostering, and that's when I saw Rusty.

He was really shy, and I was immediately drawn

to how he seemed to be so scared of the world but became happy and playful when showered with attention.

Mrs. Rose had named him Rusty for his reddish-brown fur, and she told me that a hiker had found him abandoned in the woods, hiding under some rocks.

It took some convincing, but eventually Mom and Dad decided that having a dog in the house would be a great addition to the family, and we adopted Rusty.

I quickly found out that adopting a cute dog is a lot more work than actually taking care of one—Rusty needs to be walked twice a day, and picking up his poop is never fun.

But I love that little guy to pieces, and whenever he hops up onto my bed and curls up into a bagel to take a nap, I smile. And even though I'm cleaning up after him constantly, I wouldn't trade him for anything.

Rusty is the family dog, though, and if Kelsey wanted to spend some time with him, that was awesome.

"All right," I told Kelsey. "Maybe Jenna will want to go for a run with me."

Jenna is my older sister. She mostly keeps to her own group of friends, but every once in a while she'll hang out with Kelsey and me.

When we got home, Rusty was waiting for us at the door. After wrapping him in a giant hug and rubbing his furry brown head while he wagged his tail happily, I took off my school shoes and padded in socks to the kitchen, where Dad was waiting for us with after-school snacks.

"I present to you ... apple nachos!" he said proudly, displaying a plate covered in thinly cut apples slices arranged carefully in a spiral. He had drizzled peanut butter, honey, and granola over them.

"Cool!" I washed my hands with soap and water, then picked up a slice and gobbled it up.

"This is great, Dad!" I mumbled as I picked up three more slices and fit them all in my mouth.

"Agreed," Kelsey said, her mouth equally full.

"Did you get this recipe from Grandpa and Nans?" I asked, licking peanut butter off my finger.

My grandparents are both really talented cooks and have owned a restaurant called the Park View Table in our little town of Bellgrove since basically forever.

It's a family operation, with pretty much all my relatives helping out in one way or another—including Kelsey, Jenna, and me.

I've got four cousins who also work there, and together we make sure that the floors are swept, the tables are bused, the orders are right, and that things run as smoothly as possible.

My grandmother's specialty is donuts, and years ago she created a counter inside the restaurant called Donut Dreams that my uncle Mike runs now.

Nans has always had a way of making something ordinary extraordinary—like taking a chocolate donut and making it extra chocolatey by adding a chocolate glaze and chocolate cream inside.

Anyway, I figured that if my dad was sprucing up our snacks, he must have gotten it from a secret family recipe.

"Nope," Dad said, surprising me. "I got it off the old Internet. Grandpa and Nans are too busy planning for Jazz Fest to share recipes right now."

The Bellgrove Jazz Fest is seriously one of the busiest times of the entire year for our family.

Every fall, our whole town gets together the third Saturday after Labor Day to celebrate jazz music with a huge festival that's set up along Main Street.

In addition to an awesome parade and good music, local restaurants set up a ton of food booths so we can eat their tasty food outdoors. We have a parade and food booths at Jazz Fest and other town celebrations too. And Bellgrove loves to end any festival with a bonfire at the lake. Our festival days may be kind of similar, but they're all still really fun.

We've got a Donut Dreams booth, and we usually sell out of donuts every year. Last year, we even had a giveaway—if you're able to answer a trivia question about jazz, you got a free donut!

"Well, these apple nachos are still delicious, even if it wasn't something that was handed down over generations. Thanks, Dad!"

I downed the rest of my snack and went to my room to change.

On my way, I stopped by the living room, where I found Jenna in front of the TV, watching a movie and eating popcorn.

She doesn't have much free time to just chill because she's usually playing tennis, taking piano lessons, or working at the Park. So when she does have time to relax, she really savors it.

8

"Hey, Jenna. Want to go on a run with me?" I asked hopefully.

"Nope." Jenna's eyes were glued to the screen, where a pretty exciting car chase was happening. "I would never keep up."

I laughed. "Of course you would. You're, like, at least three inches taller than I am."

"Doesn't matter," said Kelsey, coming into the room with Rusty at her heels. "You're way too fast for the both of us, Molly."

"Yeah, plus running is no fun at all," Jenna said. "It's just flopping one foot in front of the other over and over again. It's monotonous and boring."

I winced.

I've heard this argument before. I can't say that running is the most glamorous of things to be doing on a Monday afternoon.

"I know it can look boring," I told my sisters. "But it's really important for me to stay in shape for soccer, and running is the best thing I can do to make sure that I'm competitive on the field."

Jenna shot me a look that definitely had a big-sister-does-not-want-to-be-bothered air to it.

"Molly, I appreciate that you love soccer. I really

do. But I'm not going on a run, and right now I want to watch my movie."

"All right," I sighed, and headed upstairs with Kelsey.

"Hey, Molly," Kelsey said as she paused in front of her bedroom door. "You know, I really admire how dedicated you are to soccer."

I had been feeling pretty glum at Jenna being annoyed at me, but Kelsey's words cheered me up.

"You do?"

"Yeah." Kelsey grinned. "You've got a lot of perseverance. And even though I am also not ever going to go running with you, it's really awesome that you're doing something that you love."

"Thanks, Kelsey." I impulsively gave her a hug. "Soccer does mean a lot to me. One day I'm hoping that it'll get me a sports scholarship into college. Stanford or University of North Carolina would be great, but I would settle for UCLA if I had to."

"Well, while you figure out your life plans five years from now, I'm going to go read my book."

Kelsey hugged me back, then went into her room, while I went into mine.

I changed into my running shorts—pale pink

with black stripes—and a dark green sleeveless shirt.

Even though it was fall, I loved the feeling of the wind on my shoulders when I was outside and pumping my legs as hard as I could.

I used a scrunchie to tie my hair back into a long ponytail, then went downstairs to grab a big glass of water.

After gulping it down, I yelled out to my dad, who was in the living room with Jenna. "I'm going for a run!"

"Have fun, sweetie," he called back.

I went to the front door and pulled my running sneakers from the shoe cubby. I sat down and laced up them up.

I loved this part right before I headed out the door. I liked to get the tension of the laces just right against my feet, tight but not too tight, until each sneaker felt like it was an extension of my own foot.

I stood up, checked the time, then headed out.

On the front steps I breathed in the cool air while I did a couple of stretches. Then I took off at an easy jog. After a couple of minutes, I gradually increased my pace, feeling my heart rate ramp up.

By the time I reached the track, I could feel my

heart pounding. There was sweat rolling down the sides of my temples, and despite the chill air, I was warm.

My foot hit the rubber of the track, and like a switch that had suddenly been flipped on, I burst into my highest gear. I glided across the ground, feeling only my body and my heart and my determination as I pushed myself to the limit.

What I love about running is that there comes a moment, after all the groans and protests that your muscles make, when everything seems to melt away. Your mind quiets, and while you're still working like crazy to run, it all feels effortless and beautiful.

I finished my run and checked my time on my watch.

I'd run a mile on the track in eight minutes!

It was one of the best times I had ever gotten. I felt excited and happy and strong.

In a lot of ways, running for me was a means to an end. It steadied me, and I liked how it was part of my daily life.

But I mostly ran because it helped me with my stamina while playing soccer, which was absolutely the most important thing in my life besides family.

And I was going to need a lot of stamina soon.

My soccer team, the Falcons, was having a really big match in two weeks, and I had to be in tip-top shape if I wanted our team to have a chance at winning.

Chapter Two
The Talent Scout

The next morning I woke up feeling great. Last night's run had been wonderful, and Dad had made one of my favorite meals for dinner—veggie kebabs cooked over the grill, served with roasted corn and potatoes.

I rolled out of bed and went to the bathroom to brush my teeth.

As I did, I passed Jenna in the hallway.

"Might want to check your phone," she told me. "It's been pinging off the hook."

Mom and Dad have a rule in the house: no phones in bed. Every night before we go to sleep, we set our phones on a table downstairs in the family room and plug them into their chargers.

Sometimes I'm really tempted to sneak down and see if I've gotten any messages from my friends, but I know that my parents' rule exists because they don't want us to worry about something that we find out right before we're supposed to go to sleep.

I ran my toothbrush over my teeth and splashed cold water on my face.

Then I hurried back to my room to pack my soccer duffel. Cleats, socks, uniform, water bottle, extra hair scrunchie in case mine broke—everything went into the bag.

Once I was done, I changed for school and raced down the stairs to check my phone.

There were seven texts from my friend Madeline, or Maddy for short:

OMG I have BIG news.

I can't wait to tell you.

I would tell you over text

But it's just too important.

And I want to tell you in person.

I'll meet you at your locker.

HURRY.

Maddy and I have been BFFs since preschool, and we've been playing soccer together for just as long.

On the field, it's almost as though we can read each other's minds. I can tell by the way she dribbles or runs whether or not she's going to pass or shoot the ball.

We both play offense: Maddy's a striker, which means she is always looking for ways to score, while I'm the attacking midfielder, which means I'm constantly trying to set Maddy up to score.

Sometimes I get a shot or two on the goal during a game, but I really like the work of hanging in the midfield, trying to outwit the other team's players and intercepting the ball as they pass it between themselves.

My speed is my weapon—a lot of times the other team misjudges how fast I can move.

They don't know how seriously I take soccer, and

how dedicated I am to running almost every day so that out on the field, when I want to get somewhere quickly, I do.

Maddy and I don't share a lot of classes together, so I'm guessing that whatever news she's got has something to do with soccer.

I gathered up my backpack and soccer duffel, and ate a hasty breakfast of buttery toast.

Just as I finished, Kelsey came into the kitchen to get her own breakfast. Jenna was already on her way out the door.

"Kelsey, I'm going to school early today to meet up with Maddy," I told my sister as I gulped down a quick glass of orange juice. "Want to come with?"

Kelsey shook her head and rubbed her eyes. "I finished my book late last night. Too tired to go anywhere in a rush right now."

"Did it have a good ending?" I asked her.

She smiled. "The best. I think I'm going to read more by the same author. I love her writing."

I nodded and walked out the door. Half walking, half jogging, I got to school in record time and headed for my locker.

As promised, Maddy was waiting for me there.

"Molly!" Maddy was so excited she could barely hold her feet still. She swayed back and forth with glee. "I've got something to tell you!"

"Spill!" I said, fiddling with my combination lock until it clicked open.

"So I ran into Coach Wendy yesterday when I was leaving school. And guess what she said?" Maddy jumped up and down.

Coach Wendy is the soccer coach for the Falcons. She's really great at encouraging the team, even if we're losing by a lot.

I think I'm a little more competitive than the rest of my teammates, and sometimes I wish she would drive us a little harder, but I do love that no matter how any game ends, she always makes us feel like we did our best.

I dropped my soccer duffel into my locker and turned to Maddy.

"Does it have to do with our big game against the Tigers in two weeks?"

Maddy nodded happily. "Yeah!"

"Did Coach Wendy find out something that we need to be worried about?"

It looked like Maddy was really happy about her

news, but I was cautious. I wanted to be prepared if Coach Wendy had found out that the Tigers had a secret weapon—like a really good play, or a goalie who had never let a shot go into the net.

"Nope. This is different—and better." Maddy took a deep breath. "Coach Wendy's sister Annie is in town. She's also into soccer, and in a big way. She was a college soccer coach for a couple of years, but she just changed jobs and now she's a scout!"

"Wait. Does that mean . . ."

A flash of nervousness went through my stomach.

"Yup." Maddy did a little dance. "Annie is going to be at our match against the Tigers. And she's going to watch us play!"

I couldn't believe it.

I love having the energy of the audience in the bleachers when I'm playing, but in all the years that I've played soccer, there has never been a professional watching me from the sidelines.

"That's awesome news!" I said, then stopped. "But that's also kind of scary. What if we mess up while she's watching?"

Maddy laughed. "You? Mess up? Molly, you're the best player on the team. You're going to do great."

"Thanks," I said, but my stomach was still fluttering.

As I closed my locker and reset my combination lock, I couldn't help thinking that maybe I'm good at soccer because I've been able to concentrate on just the game.

With someone important watching, I wasn't sure how well I was going to play.

Classes that day went by in a blur. Usually, I can pay attention to my teachers, but I kept getting distracted by Maddy's news. Luckily, I didn't have any tests that day.

Once lunch rolled around, I met up with Maddy again. We went through the lunch line and then sat at our usual table in the cafeteria.

Normally I'm really hungry, but today I picked at my turkey and cheese sandwich. My belly felt like it was constantly on a roller coaster, even though I was sitting perfectly still.

"Are you still thinking about Coach Wendy's sister being at our game?" Maddy asked.

I looked down at my food and sighed.

"Yeah. I mean, we don't know why she's going to be there—maybe she just wants to see her sister in action. But I can't help thinking that if I can make a good impression, maybe that will make me one step closer to my goal of getting into college on a soccer scholarship."

"Well, that just means we'll have to be extra good at the game then."

Maddy bit into an apple and nudged me gently, trying to shake me out of my weird mood.

"Don't worry, Molly. You've been practicing so hard all season long, and really since we were five. We've been on a huge winning streak. And I hear the Tigers aren't that bad to play. Everything will be fine."

I grinned at my best friend.

"Thanks, Maddy," I said. "You're really good at making me feel better."

"Anytime." Maddy grinned back. "Want to hear a good joke?"

I laughed even before I heard the punch line. "Sure."

"How many tickles does it take to tickle an octopus?" Maddy asked me.

I thought about it for a minute, then shook my head. "I have no idea."

"Ten. Ten tickles!" Maddy crowed.

"Ten? Ten . . . ooh. Tentacles!" I groaned, but it quickly turned into a giggle.

Maddy really was the best friend a person could have.

We finished up lunch and said goodbye to one another.

The rest of the afternoon raced by, and when the final bell rang, I headed to the locker room to change for soccer practice.

It used to be that I had time to go home and grab a snack, and then Dad would drive me to soccer.

It was a nice break between school and practice, but Coach Wendy soon realized that a lot of the girls were staying at the school and waiting around with nothing to do until practice because they didn't have time to go home.

A few weeks after the season started, she told us that practice would happen half an hour after school ended, which gave us enough time to change into our uniforms and get out on the field.

Even though Dad doesn't have to attend my soccer practices anymore, he still drives over to the soccer field and supports me from the bleachers.

He's been to pretty much all my games and is

just as excited about soccer as I am. But he's not one of those parents who are constantly yelling to their kid and encouraging them, which can get kind of annoying after a while.

My dad's more the kind of person who doesn't really yell, but afterward while driving home he might compliment me on a really good play that I did, or something that wasn't flashy but still took a lot of skill to do.

When I got to the field, my dad was just arriving. As he got out of the car, I ran over to him and gave him a hug.

"Good day at school, Molly?" he asked me.

"Eh, it was pretty normal. But I'm ready to stretch my legs and do some drills," I replied.

"That's my girl."

Dad kissed me on the top of my head, then went over to the bleachers.

I ran back onto the field, where a couple of girls on the team had gathered.

Isabella was there, sitting on the grass and stretching her hands out toward her toes. I think of Isabella as one of my good friends and I love spending time with her, but I'm not as close to her as I am to Maddy.

"Hey, Isabella," I greeted her.

"Molly! Got a question for you." Isabella finished her stretch and stood up. "My mom is taking me to the mall this Saturday. Want to come along?"

"Sure!"

As much as I loved soccer and running and being outside, the thought of having a girls' day out at the mall sounded awesome.

"Do you think we can invite Maddy?" I asked.

I wasn't sure whether Isabella wanted to go with just me, but anything that included Maddy would make things that much better.

"Yeah!" Isabella replied. "We've got plenty of room in the car."

"Yay!"

The butterflies in my stomach were momentarily replaced with a jolt of excitement. Spending the day looking at fun things sounded like the perfect plan to get my mind off Coach Wendy's sister.

Just then one of our soccer mates, Riley, jogged over.

Riley is really good friends with Kelsey. Sometimes I think Kelsey shares more with Riley than she does with me, which can feel weird, since Kelsey is my own sister. But they do have a lot more in common.

When Riley joined our team earlier this year, she had to work through a lot of nervousness because she wasn't used to playing with any of us. She messed up a lot, both in practice and in games.

I didn't really like the fact that our team felt out of sync with a new player who wasn't used to our strategies, but Coach Wendy kept encouraging Riley, and worked with Maddy and me to include her in our plays.

In our last game, we did the same play over and over again, passing the ball to Riley until she finally made a goal!

Even though we lost that game 8–2, it did feel pretty cool to help a teammate believe in herself and be able to work through her fears to score for the team.

"Hey, did you hear about Coach Wendy's sister?" I asked Riley and Isabella.

Both girls shook their heads.

I quickly explained what Maddy had told me. Just as I finished, Maddy joined us along with the rest of the team.

Riley and Isabella asked Maddy a few more questions, trying to find out more about Annie, but everything she knew she had already told me, and I had already told them.

We warmed up together, running in place, stretching, lunging, and getting our muscles ready before working on drills. Right before warm-ups ended, I decided that I wanted to find out more about this mysterious person coming to our game against the Tigers. I jogged over to Coach Wendy. She was holding a clipboard and tapping her pen against it.

"Hey, Coach, do you have time for a quick question?" I asked.

Coach Wendy looked up from her clipboard. "Sure, Molly. What's up?"

"Maddy told me that your sister Annie is coming to our game in two weeks. Is that really true?"

The coach's face broke out into a smile. "It's a hundred percent true," she told me. "In fact, I should make this announcement to the whole team."

She lifted up a whistle that was hanging around her neck and blew it. "Girls, gather around!" she called.

When the team was assembled, Coach Wendy tucked her clipboard under her arm and addressed everyone.

"I have always said that it doesn't matter whether we win or lose when we're out there, it's how we play as a team. As long as you all work together and support each other, I consider each and every one of our games a success."

She paused. "That being said, I want to tell you about some exciting news I heard last night. My sister Annie is coming to visit in a couple of weeks. She's a talent scout for college soccer and has heard a lot about the Falcons from me. She's interested in coming to our game against the Tigers."

A murmur went through the group.

We all looked at one another and shuffled our feet. Maddy, Isabella, Riley, and I all knew, but some of the team was hearing this for the first time.

"Will she be doing any scouting at the game?" I asked Coach Wendy.

It was the big question that I think was on everybody's minds.

Or maybe it was just on my mind. If we were being scouted, out of our whole team, I think I would be the most excited—and nervous—about it.

"Annie's mostly going for fun," Coach Wendy told us.

Relief and disappointment flooded through me at the same time. It was an odd feeling.

All the pressure I had expected to feel about being watched by a scout was suddenly gone, but in the back of my head, I realized that I was secretly hoping Coach Wendy's sister would get me one step closer to going to college on a soccer scholarship.

"I say *mostly*," Coach Wendy said, as if she was reading my mind. "She also wants to see which players show promise for the future. You are all still in middle school and are five years away from even thinking about college, but Annie has always liked to plan ahead. If any of you really impress her, she's going to remember you."

And just like that, a big rock of nervousness landed with a thud at the bottom of my belly.

Coach Wendy was looking right at me, and even though she was smiling, I felt like all of a sudden a huge spotlight had been turned on all of us, and wouldn't go off until after the game.

"Molly, isn't that awesome?" Maddy nudged me. "If we work really hard, maybe Coach Wendy's sister will remember us when we're seniors and looking for soccer scholarships."

I swallowed hard and nodded.

"That means we're going to have to practice really hard over the next couple of weeks," I said.

Maddy grinned. "I'm up for it if you are."

Coach Wendy blew her whistle, and we started our drills. We ran short sprints, then did some dribbling drills, where we moved the ball back and forth between a line of cones. After that, we moved on to a zigzag dribbling drill that had us working the ball in a winding pattern all over the field that was a lot of fun.

By that time, a lot of the team was starting to get out of breath. But I was still feeling really good. All that running had built up my endurance, and instead of being tired, it was like all my muscles were just starting to wake up. Next, we practiced passing. Maddy and I normally team up together, but today we invited Isabella to join us. We formed a triangle and began kicking and passing the ball to one another.

"Oh!" Isabella said when we were done with the drill. "Hey, Maddy, do you want to come shopping with Molly and me on Saturday?"

"I have to ask my mom, but I would love to!" Maddy replied.

"Great!" I said, then laughed. "I should probably ask my dad, too."

We finished up our practice with three-on-three scrimmages, which were great because it meant that everyone got a chance to practice their skills, since there were a lot fewer players on the field than if there were two whole teams playing.

After we were done, Coach Wendy dismissed us. I grabbed my things and went over to my dad, who was getting down from the bleachers.

"Hey, Dad. Can I go to the mall with Isabella and Maddy this weekend?" I asked him.

"As long as Mom agrees, I'm okay with it," Dad said.

It only took a second to text Mom and get her to say yes.

I ran over to Isabella and Maddy to tell them the news, then got into the car with my dad to drive home.

As we were going down the street, I told him all about Coach Wendy's sister.

"Honey, that's great news!" Dad said. "But you also shouldn't feel like this is your only chance to make an impression. There's plenty of time left for you to grow into your role as the Falcons' number one soccer star of all time."

I smiled. "Thanks, Dad."

I felt really lucky to have a parent who supported my dreams.

Chapter Three
The Girl at the Mall

The rest of the week went by quickly, and before long, Saturday morning arrived.

When Kelsey heard that I was going to the mall, she wanted to go too. Then she wanted to invite Riley, but there wasn't enough room in Isabella's car to hold all five of us.

So instead, Isabella's mom picked me up at my house and Maddy at hers, while Kelsey got a ride from Riley's dad to the mall.

Once we got there and Isabella's mom had parked, we spilled out of the back seat and rushed toward the mall entrance.

There were a lot of different places to go in, but we always liked to get as close as we could to the east entrance, near where a bunch of our favorite shops were located.

Once we got inside, Kelsey and Riley headed off to check out a big sneaker sale.

The mall was shaped like a huge rectangle, with two different floors and a food court right in the middle. Our first stop was Rebel Girls, a clothing shop that had a great selection for tweens like us.

I picked out a striped pink-and-green V-neck sweater, while Maddy found a pair of blue jeans that fit her perfectly.

Isabella didn't find anything she wanted, but she struck gold when we went to Kelly's, a jewelry and accessories store (it doesn't have super-expensive stuff that you find in fancy places, but we still loved how pretty everything looked), and she found a pair of earrings that matched her eyes.

"Hey, I have an idea," Maddy said as we were heading to the food court for lunch. "Want to get matching nail polish and wear it for the big game against the Tigers?"

"Sure!" I said.

I liked the idea of feeling even more like a team by coordinating our colors.

"What do you think of finding a shade of red that matches our uniforms?" I asked.

Our uniforms are red and white, which are my school's colors.

"That's a great idea, Molly!" Isabella pointed to the glass window-front display of the store next to us. It had tons of different colors of nail polish lined up in little bottles. "Let's go there!"

We went in and spent the next ten minutes comparing different bottles of polish.

Finally, Isabella held up a bottle of pretty red nail polish that looked like it matched our uniform perfectly.

"What do you think about this one?" she asked.

"That's great—I think we should get it!" I said.

But just as I said it, another bottle caught my eye. It was pretty much the same color as the bottle that Isabella had, only it had glitter.

I grabbed it off the shelf and held it up to Isabella and Maddy.

"Yes!" they both shouted at once.

After we paid for our bottles of identical polish, it was time for lunch. We were starving so we all made a beeline for the food court and got slices of pizza and soda, then sat at a table with Isabella's mom to eat.

Halfway through our meal, we heard the sound of a ringtone. Isabella's mom dipped her hand in her purse and pulled out her phone. She looked at the screen, then turned to us.

"Girls, I have to take this call. I'll be right over there," she said, pointing to a corner of the food court that had a lot fewer people in it and looked like it would be less noisy.

"Okay, we'll be here," said Isabella, taking a giant bite of pizza. She swallowed and took a sip of soda and then smiled at her mom. "We've still got tons of food to eat, so take your time."

"I'll just be a few minutes." Isabella's mom gave her a quick kiss on the head, then hurried away, her phone to her ear.

The rest of us continued chatting and eating, talking about school and soccer.

We were almost done with our slices when I saw a group of three girls coming our way. They were all about our age and were laughing and joking with one another as they carried trays full of salad in their hands.

As they sat down next to us, I noticed that they all

had matching bracelets around their wrists. Each of the bracelets had a tiny tiger charm on it.

"Hey, I recognize them." Isabella's voice had dropped to a whisper. "My cousin goes to school with them, and I've seen them over at her house. They play for the Tigers."

She glanced really quickly at them, and then turned back to us. "See the girl with the short blond hair in the blue shirt?"

I looked over and saw the girl that Isabella was mentioning. She was small and sturdy and was forking a piece of lettuce into her mouth. She looked right back at me, a big smirk on her face.

I jerked my head back to the table with my friends. "I see her."

"Well, her name is Jodie Perkins, and she's an attacking midfielder, just like you, Molly." Isabella took a deep breath. "She's also the best player on the team. My cousin says that her mom used to be a professional soccer player, and that Jodie has been playing soccer since she was three."

Suddenly, the pizza that I had been enthusiastically chomping down on didn't taste so great. Not only was Jodie my direct competition on the field, but she also had at least two years of soccer practice on me, since I only started when I was five.

If we played the Tigers and Jodie was so good that she made our team look like dirt, Coach Wendy's sister wouldn't care how well I played. She'd be looking at the rival team, seeing their moves, and writing down Jodie's name as someone to contact in a few years.

My mouth ran dry. I took a sip of soda to try and make it feel better, but it didn't help.

Instead I stood up abruptly and went to throw my paper plate into the trash can.

As I was returning to Maddy and Isabella, I passed Jodie and her two teammates. Jodie stared at me with a gaze that was so intense I swear she was trying to see the back of my eyeballs.

"Hey," she called as I drew near. "Aren't you Molly?"

I frowned. I didn't expect to be recognized by this stranger.

"Yeah," I said. "How did you know my name?"

"My parents and I go to the Park every once in a while," Jodie said. She grinned but somehow it didn't seem friendly. "I've seen you there busing tables."

I took a closer look and realized that I had seen

Jodie at my grandparents' restaurant before. She probably knew my name because I always wore my name tag when I was working.

A knot formed in my stomach. A memory came back to me, of Jodie's mom sending back a plate of food that she said was too salty. She had treated my sister Jenna as if it was her fault that the dish wasn't something that she liked. I still remembered the hurt look on Jenna's face. It had been an uncomfortable moment—one that I wasn't too happy to remember.

"Anyway, didn't you say that you were playing for the Falcons at your school?" Jodie asked.

The knot tightened as I also remembered how friendly I had tried to be when Jodie and her family had just arrived, and how her dad had asked if I went to Jodie's school.

I had answered no, but had blurted out the school I went to, and that I loved to play soccer there.

The too-salty food, the awkward apology I made for it, and the fact that Jodie's parents hadn't left any tip on the bill came afterward.

I nodded and tried to duck away to rejoin my friends, but Jodie interrupted me before I could begin to leave.

"Well, I play for the Tigers. We've got a game against you next week," she said.

I wanted to say something cool and casual, like, *Well, may the best team win*, but somehow my voice didn't seem to want to work right.

When I finally found it, all I said was, "Mm-hmm."

Jodie held up her wrist, showing her bracelet off.

"See this?" she asked. The tiny tiger charm shimmered under the fluorescent mall lights. "All my soccer teammates have one. Katie, show Molly yours."

The girl next to Jodie, with thick red hair and glasses, held her hand up. Her bracelet slid down to rest a few inches down her wrist.

"Sasha, hold up yours," Jodie instructed.

The girl sitting across from Jodie, who had dark brown hair and freckles, showed her bracelet.

"These are our good-luck charms," Jodie told me. "But we really don't need them, because we're awesome and we're going to kick your butts at the game!"

"Don't be so sure of that," said a familiar voice behind me.

I looked over my shoulder and saw Maddy standing right behind me, and Isabella next to her. They had come over to defend me!

"Yeah, you have no idea how good we are," said Isabella.

Jodie raised her eyebrows. "You're right. I don't. But since I'm on the Tigers' team this year, you girls don't stand a chance. I bet I could dribble circles around all of you with my eyes closed."

Maddy shook her head. "I would take that bet, especially if you were up against Molly."

She looked at me and smiled. "She cares about soccer more than anyone I know."

Jodie laughed. "Caring about something and being good at something are two different things." She stood up. "Katie, Sasha, let's go."

As they left, Jodie leaned over and whispered something to her teammates. Then she looked directly at me and giggled loudly as they all walked past.

Sasha and Katie looked at me a little apologetically and didn't laugh, but they also didn't say a word as they left.

I was so mad, but also embarrassed at the same time. I didn't know what Jodie had said, but I was pretty sure that she was making fun of me.

"Molly? You all right?" Maddy touched my arm.

I bit my lip and nodded, but it was really hard to

hold back a couple of tears that threatened to spill down my cheeks.

"Forget about Jodie." Isabella came up to me and gave me a hug.

Maddy joined in on the hug, and even though I felt rotten, I had to smile. It was comforting to be surrounded by my friends, being supported and loved.

In the corner of the food court, I saw Isabella's mom tuck her phone in her purse and head toward us.

"Sorry about that," she said when she reached us. "Ready to do more shopping, or are you girls done for the day?"

"I think I'm ready to leave," Isabella said.

"Me too," said Maddy.

"Me three," I said.

As Isabella's mom led the way to the exit, Maddy, Isabella, and I hung back a little bit.

"Are you sure you're okay?" Maddy asked me.

"Yeah. But I wish I knew what Jodie said about me to Sasha and Katie," I said.

Isabella shook her head. "Ignore her. She just likes to be mean for mean's sake."

We got to the car and unloaded the things we had

bought into the trunk. As we buckled our seat belts, Maddy and Isabella talked about how excited they were to have matching glittery red nails.

I wanted to join in, but my mind kept on drifting back to Jodie.

What if she was right?

What if the Tigers were so good, and she was so good, that the Falcons ended up looking terrible in our big game against them?

Chapter Four
The Turquoise Coat

By the time Isabella's mom dropped me off, the temperature had lowered a lot. Even though it took me only a few seconds to get from the car to my front door, I was already shivering in the thin coat that I had worn to the mall.

I ran to my room and quickly threw on my new sweater to warm up. It looked just as good as it had in the dressing room of Rebel Girls, but somehow it didn't seem as special to me as when I had bought it.

I realized that Jodie was really getting to me. I had to snap out of it. Isabella and Maddy were right—it was best to try and ignore her. After all, worrying about what she'd said wasn't going to do me any good.

I went to see if Kelsey had already come home from her own shopping trip with Riley. She had, and she showed me a few new headbands that she had gotten.

I tried to pay attention, but I was still kind of distracted by running into Jodie and couldn't quite focus.

I did some homework, throwing myself into my history textbook, until dinnertime.

When I went down to the kitchen to eat, Dad was there, serving out bowls of Portuguese kale soup along with slices of freshly made bread.

"How was the mall?" he asked me.

"It was . . . fine," I said. "But I ran into this girl Jodie, who recognized me from the Park. She's not very nice. She's on the Tigers' soccer team, and I'm not looking forward to facing off against her in our big match next week."

Dad frowned. "I'm sorry to hear that, Molly. Do you want to talk about it?"

I thought about it, then shook my head.

"I already kind of worked it out with Maddy and Isabella. But thanks, Dad."

"Anytime, sweetie. You can always come to me for anything."

Dad handed me two bowls of soup to take to the table.

"I know."

I helped Dad carry the soup bowls to the table, then set up silverware, napkins, and glasses of water. Already the smell of the soup was making my mouth water. I love it when Dad cooks. And this soup was just what I needed—something warm and filling.

"Dinnertime!" Dad called.

Kelsey came down from her room, and Jenna and Mom came in from the living room. After we all sat down, we went around the table and shared what had happened during our day.

Jenna complimented my new sweater, and I told my family about the nail polish Maddy, Isabella, and I had gotten.

"Wait," said Kelsey. "So, the three of you are going to wear it to the big game, but no one else? Doesn't that make you, like, a little cliquey since no one else on your team is going to be wearing it?"

"Well, it's also a friend thing," I said slowly. "But I see your point."

"Maybe you should ask Riley if she wants to paint her nails too," Kelsey suggested. It wasn't a bad idea.

I would feel pretty terrible if Riley felt left out when she noticed that her soccer friends were wearing something they had obviously coordinated with one another, and she wasn't included.

"You're right," I said to Kelsey. "I will. And what's more, I'm going to ask the whole team if they all want to paint their nails. I mean, we're in this together."

Mom nodded approvingly.

"I think that's a great idea, Molly. And thank you for bringing that up, Kelsey."

She buttered a piece of bread and dunked it into her soup. Once she had finished eating the bread, she began telling us about her day.

"I was at the library talking to the town librarian, Ms. Castro," she said. "She's organizing a huge clothing drive tomorrow, where they'll be collecting warm clothes and coats for families in need before winter arrives."

"That's a great cause," Dad said. "And it's a good thing they're doing it now. I was surprised at how cold it got today, and it's only going to get colder for the next couple of months."

"Yeah, I'm going to need to change out my wardrobe," I said.

Twice a year, I swap out almost all the clothes in my closet, depending on how warm it is.

Back in April, I packed up all my warm clothes—jackets and coats, sweaters, thick socks, long pants, and hoodies—into three huge suitcases and pushed them into storage under my bed. Right now, my closet was full of summer dresses and shorts, but they weren't the most practical things to wear in fifty-degree weather.

"Before you do that, would you consider donating some of your winter clothes to the clothing drive?" Mom asked me.

I hesitated. I do really love my clothes, and it's hard to give up the outfits that I've personally chosen over the years.

But there were a lot of things that I'd been on the verge of outgrowing last year. Plus, I'd had a growth spurt over the summer and had grown close to two inches.

I nodded at Mom. "I bet I've got a lot of stuff that would no longer fit me. I'd be happy to donate them. And I can even donate outfits that do fit, but I don't wear very often. If it helps kids in need, I'm happy to do it."

"Thanks, Molly," Mom said, smiling warmly at

me. She turned to Kelsey, then Jenna. "Anyone else?"

Kelsey said yes too. It took a little more prodding to get Jenna to agree to donate clothes—she insisted that everything she owned was special and she needed all her clothes, but eventually she did agree to give up a few pairs of pants and sweaters.

After dinner, Kelsey and I helped clear dishes while Jenna loaded the dishwasher. When we were done, we all headed to our rooms to sort through our clothes and figure out which ones we wanted to donate.

I pulled out my suitcases and unzipped them fully, lifting the flaps clear of the neatly stacked piles of clothes inside.

There was a knock at my door.

"Come in!" I called.

Mom came into my bedroom holding a cardboard box that was about the size of one of my suitcases. She set it down next to me.

"You can put your donations here," she said.

I peered out in the hallway and saw two more boxes that were about the same size as the one that Mom had given me.

"Wait. Are those for me too?"

Mom laughed. "They're for Kelsey and Jenna. I'm not expecting you to give up all your clothes, Molly."

"Whew," I said as Mom went back into the hallway to knock on Kelsey's and Jenna's doors.

It was easy to give up half a dozen pair of pants where the hems came halfway up my shins and a few sweaters where my arms stuck out of the sleeves way too far.

I also had a few shirts with small mustard or ketchup stains on them that wouldn't come out no matter how many times I had run them through the wash. The stains didn't show too much, so I was comfortable donating those shirts as well.

As I rummaged through my suitcases, I came across a few pairs of yoga pants and leggings that I threw into the box. They were worn, and although they didn't have holes, they were pretty thin at the knees.

When I was finished sorting through the clothes that I wanted to donate, my suitcases were empty. I filled them up with my summer clothes, then began to hang my winter clothes in my closet.

I was nearly done when I came across my favorite winter coat. It was a bright turquoise and made from synthetic down, which I thought was awesome because it kept me super warm, but it didn't have actual goose feathers in it like a real down coat.

I held the coat up to my face and pressed my cheek into a sleeve. I'd been wearing this coat for the past two years, and I always felt protected against the winter in it.

It was big enough, too, that even with my growth spurt, it still fit.

I started to hang it up in my closet, when I stopped. I looked at the rest of my coats hanging up. I had three of them.

None of them were as good as my turquoise winter coat. But all of them still fit. And all of them would still protect me from the cold.

I pulled the coat off the hanger and put it on one last time, feeling its soft, comforting warmth.

As much as I loved it, the thought of giving it to someone who would appreciate just as much, if not more, than I had made me fold it up carefully and place it into my box of donations. At this point it was pretty much full.

Mom entered my room, a roll of packing tape in her hand. "You all set, Molly?" she asked me.

I pointed to the box and nodded. "Just added my last piece."

Mom saw the flash of turquoise at the top of the box. Her eyes softened. "Oh, honey, you don't have to give up your best coat."

"But I want to," I replied. "If this clothing drive is for people in need, than whoever gets this coat will really need it. I've got plenty of clothes that I love that will keep me warm this winter. But there may be a girl out there whose only coat will be this one."

Mom looked like she was about to cry, but in a good way.

"I'm really proud of you, Molly," she said. "Being generous is the best way to be."

She knelt down and was about to seal the box with the packing tape when I stopped her.

"Hold on," I said. "I want to donate just one more thing."

I quickly changed out of my new sweater that I had just gotten at the mall, swapping it out for a gray hoodie. I gave Mom the sweater.

"I bet that people who get these clothes can get a little tired of hand-me-downs. Maybe something new will brighten their day."

Mom smiled. "You know, if you wanted to help out even more, the clothing drive tomorrow could use some volunteers to help sort the donations," she said. "Would you be interested? We could go together."

I nodded. "I usually work at the Park on Sunday mornings, but I'll see if Lindsay could take my place. I'd love to help sort the donations."

"It's a date, then!" Mom said.

She held the flaps of the box open while I added my final item. She closed up the box and pulled a long strip of packing tape down on it.

"Done," she said, dusting off her hands. "Now, let's go see how far your sisters have gotten."

Kelsey's donation box was only half-full, and Jenna's was a little less than half, so Mom combined the two boxes into one. Together we helped load them in her car so they would be ready to go the next morning.

When we got back into the house, Mom looked at the clock.

"Bedtime, girls," she said.

We plugged our phones into their chargers downstairs, then all headed up the stairs to brush our teeth and tuck in for the night.

As I lay there thinking about the clothing drive, I realized that all the nervousness that I had been storing up the past couple of days was gone.

I smiled sleepily.

I was going to do some good work tomorrow, with the added bonus that I had finally found something to distract me from the big game, Coach Wendy's sister, and Jodie's mean words.

Chapter Five
Trouble at the Library

I woke up in the morning feeling excited for the day. Since I didn't know how long the clothing drive would take, I decided to go for an early run in case I would be busy until the evening.

It was definitely chilly when I stepped outside, but after ten minutes of jogging around the neighborhood, I was warm enough to be able to enjoy the bite in the air.

There's something amazing about the feel of fall, especially if you're a runner or a soccer player. It's the perfect time to be outside. The weather is usually sunny, and everything looks sharp and beautiful.

The leaves on the trees had started to change from their summer green to the reds and goldens of autumn, and as I ran by them, happiness welled in my heart.

I hit the track and did a couple of laps. I wasn't as fast as I had been earlier in the week, but that was okay. I wasn't going to pressure myself to make a personal best every single time I went out.

I got home, took a quick shower, then ate a breakfast of homemade waffles that Dad had made with our old-fashioned waffle iron. With maple syrup and sliced bananas, and a big glass of orange juice, it was the perfect breakfast.

While I was bringing my empty plate to the sink, Mom appeared in the kitchen.

"Molly, ready in five," she said.

"Yup."

I grabbed my phone, ran upstairs, quickly brushed my teeth, and then headed to the car.

Mom and I arrived at the library around ten thirty. After parking, we brought the two donation boxes downstairs to the common room, where a lot of public events take place.

The room was filled with dozens of boxes and tables piled high with clothes. A couple of volunteers were already there, sorting through them.

"I'm so glad you're here!" said Ms. Castro when she saw my mom.

I liked Ms. Castro a lot. She was an older woman with gray hair, but she loved to wear bright clothes. Today she had on a bright red dress and a yellow scarf wrapped around her neck.

She looked at me.

"Molly! What a lovely surprise. Are you volunteering as well?"

I nodded, and Ms. Castro clapped her hands.

"Wonderful." She pointed at a table in the corner. "You and your mom can do some sorting over there. Right now we're separating clothes into tops and bottoms. After that, we'll separate them into piles for men, women, girls, boys, and infants."

"Sounds good!" I told her.

Mom and I went over to the table and began to sort the clothes. We were on our fifth box, having a good time coming up with jokes to tell Dad when we got home, when I caught a glance of someone out of the corner of my eye.

My heart almost stopped. It couldn't be. Not here.

But when I turned and looked, it was.

Jodie was here.

She was on the other side of the room, sorting clothes with her mom.

All of a sudden, I didn't feel so good anymore. I couldn't believe that of all the places to be on a Sunday morning, Jodie would choose to come here.

On one hand, I guess it was kind of great that she was doing volunteer work the same as me.

On the other, I really, really, *really* didn't want to be in the same place as her.

As if she could sense me recognizing her, Jodie looked up from folding a pair of jeans and spotted me. She looked confused for a second, then nodded to me.

Not knowing what else to do, I nodded back.

Mom looked over. "Oh, isn't that Marsha Perkins?" she asked.

"I . . . um . . . I don't know?" I stammered.

"She was a huge soccer star about twenty years ago," said Mom. "And that must be her daughter."

"Yeah, we've met," I muttered.

"Molly? Is everything okay?" Mom could tell that my tone had completely changed.

"I think I just need a drink of water," I said. "My throat is kind of dry."

"I've got some water in the car. I'll go get it." Mom put down the sweater she was sorting and picked up her purse. "Or do you want to come with me?"

I shook my head. I wanted to leave, but going to the car meant crossing the room right past Jodie.

"I'll be right back," Mom promised.

Once she left, I put my head down and tried to avoid looking up again. There was a donation box at my feet and I crouched down, pulling the tape until it came off in one long peel.

I opened the box and nearly gasped when I saw my donated sweater on top of a pile of clothes. I had been so flustered at seeing Jodie that I hadn't even recognized my own donation box.

"Hi, Molly."

I jerked my head up, nearly banging it on the sorting table. "Oh. Hi, Jodie."

Jodie had her hands planted on the table and was craning her neck to look inside my donation box.

"Hey. Didn't I see you showing that sweater to your friends yesterday at the mall?"

"Uh, yeah."

While we were having lunch, Maddy, Isabella, and I had taken out all the things we had bought to look at them. I guess Jodie had been looking too.

"You just bought it, and now you're giving it away?" Jodie rolled her eyes. "How wasteful," she said.

"That's not true!" I sputtered. "I thought someone would really enjoy having something new to wear."

"Whatever." Jodie help up her hand dismissively. "You were probably not paying enough attention to that sweater to see what it really looked like. If your focus is just as bad on the soccer field, then you're going to get creamed next Sunday."

Before I could respond, she had come around the table and was digging into my donation box.

"What else are you giving away?" she asked.

I stood, frozen to the spot. I watched as she held up my favorite winter coat.

"What a lame-o color. I can see why you're giving this away," Jodie said.

She tossed it into the pile of tops.

"I'd like to sort my own clothes, please," I said, but Jodie was already holding up a pair of my yoga pants and some leggings.

"You're donating those? I would think you'd need everything to keep those skinny legs warm," she said.

She laughed, then quickly threw them on the

table and walked away before I could respond.

I didn't want to be there anymore. I raced through sorting the rest of my clothes, and by the time Mom came back, I was done with our pile.

"Can we go now?" I asked her.

Mom checked her watch, then looked around at all the people who had come out to help sort clothes. From the time we had arrived to now, about twenty other volunteers had arrived.

"I was planning on staying for another hour, but it looks like the clothing drive has enough volunteers right now. We can go home, but would you want to come back next week? The clothing drive will be here this Thursday night, too, and even though and your sisters have donated everything you want, we can still help out."

"Yeah, I can volunteer on Thursday as well. Now, can we please go?" I said quickly.

I was trying to get out of there as fast as possible, and anything that would hurry that along was fine by me.

Mom raised her eyebrows but didn't ask any questions. We gathered up our belongings and started heading toward the exit.

I walked really fast past Jodie and her mom, avoiding eye contact and ducking out into the hallway that led to the exit. Only when we were in the parking lot did I feel like I could breathe.

"Honey, what's wrong?" Mom asked. She knew immediately that something had happened.

"Can we talk about it in the car?" I asked.

I didn't want to have to face Jodie again if she suddenly popped up in the parking lot.

"Of course." Mom got her key fob out and aimed it at the car. With a beep, she unlocked it.

I jumped into the passenger seat and buckled up. I waited until we were halfway home, trying to figure out how I felt about what Jodie had said to me.

Finally I spoke up. "Mom, do you think I'm too skinny?"

Mom raised her eyebrows and shook her head. "I don't. But what makes you ask that?"

"Someone I know said that I had really skinny legs. Maybe it's a good thing that fall is here and I can keep them covered."

My mind was already racing to next summer. If it was too hot to wear pants, I would find long dresses and wear those.

Anything to keep my chicken legs hidden.

Mom stopped at a traffic light and turned to me. "Molly, there is nothing wrong with your body. You shouldn't pay any attention to anyone who says otherwise."

"You're just saying that because you're my mom." I wanted to believe her, but I didn't.

My mom was always supposed to be on my side. Maybe that meant that even if there was something wrong with my body, she wouldn't say it to my face.

Mom sighed.

"I am your mom. But I'm also telling you the truth. You're going to be going through a lot of physical changes in the next couple of years, and a lot of them aren't going to be comfortable. But as long as you're healthy, that's all that matters."

"Okay," I said.

But I didn't feel okay. When I got home, I went straight to my room to look at myself in the mirror.

I saw a tall, skinny girl looking back at me. Up until now, I had liked the way I looked. I liked the way my body moved and the things I could do with it. Like run and dribble and shoot.

But then I thought about Jodie. Her body type

was just like her mom's—small and muscular, as if her shortness concealed a powerful amount of energy that could explode at any moment into a sprint that could overtake me, or a shot on goal that I couldn't defend.

Maybe Jodie's body was better for soccer than mine was.

Maybe no matter what I did or how hard I trained, I would never be able to keep up with her because I was trapped inside arms and legs that didn't want to put on muscles.

※　※　※　※　※

Later that evening, I changed into my pajamas and got into bed. I was tired, but my brain was running everywhere, thinking about seeing Jodie at the mall, Coach Wendy's sister, Jodie's comment about my legs at the clothing drive.

There was a woof outside my door, and the scrape and scratch of a paw against wood.

My ears perked up. I knew that sound—and loved it. Rusty wanted to cuddle with me tonight!

I threw back the covers and crossed the room, then let him in. He greeted me with a wagging tail and a lick on my hand, then hopped onto the foot of the bed and settled himself down.

I stroked his head and looked down into his big brown eyes.

"You're so lucky," I told him. "You don't have to care about how you look. All you have to do is play and sleep and poop. And you don't even have to pick up your poop!"

Rusty thumped his tail.

He couldn't understand what I was saying, of course, but he was happy that I was talking to him. He laid his head on my knee.

"Love you, Rusty," I told him, scratching him behind his ears.

He looked at me with sleepy eyes and smiled.

I got back into bed and wiggled my feet down until they were next to Rusty's curled-up body. Even though he was on top of the covers and I was under them, I could still feel his warmth.

It was a comforting feeling.

Normally when Rusty stays with me, it's easy for me to sleep, but even after I closed my eyes, I kept tossing and turning while Rusty snored gently at the foot of my bed.

Donut Goals

After a while, I had only one thought, but it was enough to keep me awake for another hour before I finally drifted off to sleep.

Maybe my dreams of becoming a soccer star were just that. Dreams.

Chapter Six
Two Hundred Donuts

When I woke up on Monday morning, I could already tell it was going to be a bad day. I slept through my alarm, but I was still really tired from not being able to sleep the night before.

In the bathroom I ran out of toothpaste and found a hair on my toothbrush. It was my hair, but still. Ew.

As I got dressed for school, I glanced at myself again in the mirror, and swore that my legs had gotten skinnier.

I didn't have soccer practice today, but I did on Tuesday. Maybe I would try and do some leg exercises beforehand at the gym to build up my muscles.

I pulled on my baggiest pair of jeans and slid a black belt through the loops to keep them up. Then

I found a bulky red sweater and tossed it on before going downstairs to fix breakfast.

Aside from Rusty giving me a good-morning kiss, it was pretty much downhill from there.

I burned my breakfast toast, and halfway through walking to school, there was a sudden downpour.

Kelsey had brought her umbrella, but I had forgotten mine. She shared hers with me, but it wasn't very big, so by the time we got to school, we were each half-soaked.

My classes were okay, but I mostly kept quiet. I had lunch with Maddy as usual but found it really hard to concentrate.

When I told her about what Jodie had said to me at the clothing drive, Maddy's eyes got wide.

"Whoa. That was, like, totally out of line," she said.

"I know," I said. "But I can't stop thinking about it. This morning I looked at myself in the mirror and all I saw were stick legs. I'm way too skinny!"

"Molly, you're fine the way you are," Maddy tried to reassure me. "Jodie's just trying to scare you before our game on Sunday. She wants you to doubt yourself and feel self-conscious so you don't play as well."

I thought about it.

"Well, it's working," I said. "Now all I can think about is how my body isn't the ideal soccer player's body." I paused. "Well, that and Coach Wendy's sister. And Jazz Fest this Saturday. Agh! I'm so stressed!"

I could feel my breath coming in gasps and my heart starting to pound.

"You're hyperventilating!" Maddy handed me the paper bag from her lunch.

"Here. Put this over your mouth and take about ten short breaths," she instructed me.

I grabbed the bag and held it over my face. I did as Maddy said, and each breath got a little bit longer and calmer. By the time I was done, I felt slightly more at ease.

I handed the bag back to Maddy.

"Thanks," I said. "Where did you learn that?"

"Where I learn everything—the Internet." Maddy looked at me closely. "Do you need to go to the nurse?"

I shook my head. "I'm okay. Thanks, Maddy."

"Anytime," she replied.

The lunch bell rang. Maddy and I threw away our trash, said goodbye to one another, then headed off to our classes.

Donut Goals

I really do have the best friend in the world.

After school, it was still raining. When the weather's bad, Dad picks us up in the car. Kelsey and I met him in the school parking lot and climbed in, shaking the rain from our hair.

"How was school today, girls?" Dad asked.

"Great!" Kelsey replied. "I got a B-plus on my history test. And in art today, I learned how to sketch horses. They're really hard, but Ms. Nevins told me that my drawing was the best one in the class!"

Kelsey is super creative, and it didn't surprise me that she was the star of her art class.

A while back, she came up with an idea to make really beautiful "donut cakes" from our Donut Dreams counter, which ended up becoming a line of business at the Park called Seven Cousins Cakes—named after the seven of us cousins who work (or will work) at the restaurant.

"That's great!" Dad said.

He glanced over at me, but just for a second before returning his eyes to the road so he could concentrate on driving. "How was your day, Molly?"

"Eh." I shrugged. "Okay. But I'm feeling anxious about my soccer game this Sunday. And it's only

Monday!" I rubbed my eyes. "I just wish it could be Sunday night already and everything was over."

"But then you'd skip Saturday—and Family Fest!" Kelsey said.

Family Fest!

I couldn't believe that I had almost forgotten all about it.

One of the biggest events of the year was coming up, but all the excitement I normally feel around this time of year was being erased by the pressure of Sunday's game.

"Speaking of Family Fest, remember that it is this Friday. Which means you girls are working at the Park tonight," Dad reminded us.

Since everyone in my family like crazy on right before celebrations like Jazz Fest, Mom and Dad came up with an annual tradition to help us have fun and relax before the big day.

The Friday night before, Dad takes over Mom's shift at the Park while Mom takes Jenna, Kelsey, and me for a girls' night out.

We always go to dinner at Louie Louie, a really amazing restaurant a couple of towns over from Bellgrove that has fried ravioli and butter cake, a special Southern vanilla cake that is ooey, gooey, and oh so delicious.

Last year my cousin Lindsay ended up joining us for Family Fest, and although Kelsey and I didn't like the idea of it at first (I thought traditions were never meant to change), we ended up having a really good time.

Jenna, Kelsey, and I normally work at the Park on Friday night. But since we were taking this Friday off for Family Fest, we had to work Monday night instead.

Dad stopped by home so we could change and grab a bite to eat before we began our shifts. Once we were ready, we got back into the car along with Jenna and headed over to the restaurant.

Mom was already there, helping Grandpa and Nans out with orders.

Jenna and I grabbed aprons. Jenna quickly got to work serving tables while I did my usual job as a "runner"—running for extra napkins or ketchup or anything else a customer needed. Kelsey went behind the Donut Dreams counter to help out.

The good thing about Mondays at the Park is that they're pretty quiet. We had a number of regulars, but there was no rush like there usually is late on a Friday afternoon when I'm usually working.

Half of me expected to see Jodie's family come in, but luckily, they didn't show up and I didn't have to duck behind tables trying to avoid them.

I was really glad when the last customer was served, and Grandpa went to the entrance to change the OPEN sign to CLOSED.

I don't think I could have dealt with the stress of seeing Jodie after yesterday.

As we were wiping tables and putting chairs up for the night (not our usual jobs but tonight we were helping out with all jobs), I noticed that Grandpa was carrying around a pad of notepaper that was full of scribbles. He had been holding it all night, and whenever he had a free moment, he would sit and write something new down.

"What's that, Grandpa?" I asked when I had put the last chair on top of the table.

"This is my grand plan for Jazz Fest this year. Here, take a look." Grandpa showed me the notepad.

On the very top, he had written in all capital letters *200 DONUTS*. Below that, there was a list of different flavors that I had never heard of before:

200 DONUTS

Chocolate-glazed strawberry shortcake

Raspberry crème with almond drizzle

Very Vanilla

Blueberry waffle

Peanut butter and banana caramel

Lemon Zest Surprise

Spicy apple cider

Cinnamon Crunch

Hot cocoa

There were also a few more flavors on the list, but I couldn't quite make out what he had written, since his handwriting can be a little messy.

"Hey, Grandpa. Why did you write down '200 Donuts,' and what's this list below it?" I asked.

"Well, at last year's Jazz Fest, we donated a hundred donuts. This year I want to donate two hundred!" Grandpa grinned. "Besides the donuts we're selling, of course. It will be a lot of work, but it's going to be worth it!"

I was confused. "Why do you want to hand out so many free donuts? Won't that be two hundred donuts' worth of cash that we would be losing?"

"Haven't you ever heard the expression, 'I couldn't even give them away'? That means a product is terrible and nobody likes it, even if it's free," Grandpa explained.

"Wait . . . I still don't get it," I said. "Our donuts are really good. We should be selling them, instead of saying that they're so bad we're trying to give them away to people."

"Here's the thing," Grandpa said. "The more donuts we can give away, the more it will show me how much people like them. I hope we run out!" He grinned. Again. "It will also be a chance for us to try new flavors and find out which ones are customer favorites. I like to call it 'market research.'"

"Are the names you've written down the new flavors you want to try out?" I asked.

"They are," Grandpa replied. "In fact, Nans and I have whipped up a batch of some of them in the kitchen. Want to try some out?"

Despite having a rotten day, donuts seemed liked a pretty good way to end the night.

I went into the back, where I found Kelsey scrubbing the sink.

"Did you hear about Grandpa's experimental donuts?" I asked her.

She nodded. "He's got them over there." She pointed to a clear plastic tub full of donuts in the corner. "He told me that we could all taste-test them once our shift was over."

"Well, I'm done out front. Need any help here?" I asked Kelsey.

"Want to mop?" she asked me.

I didn't really like mopping, but I wanted to get to the donut taste testing as soon as possible, so I pulled out the mop bucket from the closet and filled it with water and a squirt of floor soap.

By the time I had swished the mop across the floor, Kelsey was done with the sink and dishes, and everyone else was finished with their work too.

Grandpa came into the kitchen and grabbed the tub. He brought it to the big stainless-steel table in the middle of the kitchen and set it down.

"Gather round—it's taste-testing time!" Grandpa called.

We all crowded around the table—Kelsey, Jenna, Mom, Nans, and me.

"Wow! Look at all these different flavors," Kelsey exclaimed. "It must have taken a lot of work. And that's on top of regular business and preparing for Jazz Fest!"

Grandpa shrugged. "It's work, but not as much as you think. Instead of making separate batches of donut dough for each flavor, we started with a big batch of my basic recipe, then divided the dough and added the different flavors at the end."

Jenna nodded. "Smart."

Grandpa opened the tub and we caught a whiff of all the donuts. They smelled heavenly. "First up— chocolate-glazed strawberry shortcake!" Grandpa announced.

He got a cutting board, then picked up a donut topped with chocolate and laid it down. Using a knife, he sliced it into six sections, then handed each of us a portion.

I popped the triangular slice of donut into my mouth. I could taste all the flavors and textures of the donut, and they were amazing.

"This is so good!" I said.

"Mmm," Jenna agreed.

"Don't change a thing," said Kelsey. "It's perfect."

We went through the donuts, one by one. I loved the raspberry crème with almond drizzle sample, but when I bit into the Very Vanilla donut, I frowned.

"Grandpa? Can I offer a suggestion?" I said.

"Yes, Molly?" Grandpa replied.

"This is pretty good . . . but I don't think it has enough vanilla in it," I said. "There's only one flavor to this donut, so I thought there would be a ton of vanilla-y flavor to it, but I can barely taste it. If I were you, I'd put at least twice the amount of vanilla extract in the batch."

"I agree with Molly that there isn't a strong flavor of vanilla, but I kind of like how subtle it is," Kelsey said. "It's almost as if it's this really nice surprise added to what you think would be a regular old-fashioned donut."

A light bulb went off in my head. "Maybe you can rename it! Instead of 'Very Vanilla,' how about 'A Hint of Vanilla'?"

Grandpa nodded approvingly. "Great idea, girls. I'm using real vanilla extract for this batch, and it can be quite expensive. 'A Hint of Vanilla' it is!"

We went through the rest of the flavors, either approving them or offering suggestions to make them better.

Grandpa scribbled down our notes on his notepad, and by the time we were done, the page was full of writing.

"This is all wonderful," he told us.

"Grandpa? Are you sure that we're not being too picky?" I asked. "That's a lot of stuff you're going to need to change before Jazz Fest. And I know it's a lot of stress just doing the whole event by itself, without having to think about perfecting new donut recipes."

Grandpa shook his head. "It's really helpful for me to hear your thoughts on these new flavors. After all, they are new, and haven't been taste-tested yet. I'd rather have honest feedback and be able to present something to our customers that I know has been approved by the family rather than trusting that I've got it right the first time when I try out something new."

"Well, now that we're all sugar-loaded, it's time to go home," Mom said, looking at the clock.

We all hugged Grandpa and Nans goodbye, then got into the car. As usual, Jenna was up front with Mom, while Kelsey and I hung out in the back seat.

"I'm glad we got to help Grandpa out, but that was a lot of donuts," said Jenna as we drove home.

She sighed. "If he has us try out any more, by the end of the week I won't be able to fit into my pants."

"What do you mean?" I asked her.

Jenna turned around from the passenger-side seat and looked at me. "Donuts have a lot of calories in them. They're one of the easiest ways to put on pounds."

She sighed. "I love the Park, and the Donut Dreams counter, and our family business, but every once in a while I wish we'd gone into making salads. Donuts are great, but I think I ate at least three whole ones tonight, and that's about two too many."

"Wait. So, if I ate a lot of donuts, I could gain weight?"

My mind started to race. Maybe if I ate donuts

constantly, my legs would fill out and then Jodie would have nothing to laugh at.

"Maybe that will help get my skinny little legs more toned for soccer."

"As much as I support your grandparents' passion for donuts, I don't think you should do that," said Mom. "Donuts would help you gain weight, but there are plenty of other foods that will help you put on muscle better. Like protein, whole grains, and lots of vegetables."

I wrinkled my nose. "Those all sound so boring."

"They can be pretty delicious, if you know how to cook them," Mom replied. "Anyway, you are not having any more donuts tonight, and since we're all a little sugared out right now, I'm going to say that tomorrow everyone should avoid sweets as well."

As we rode the rest of the way home, Kelsey started telling us about a project she was working on with Riley in history class, but I was only half paying attention.

I stared out the car window silently, looking at the darkness beyond.

In two days, I would be having my last soccer practice before the game against the Tigers on Sunday.

Due to everybody's busy schedules, we only have one soccer practice a week, but we played an extra hour before big games.

That still didn't give me a lot of time to bulk up. But I would do the best I could.

As I was thinking, a horrible thought came to me.

"Mom, does running burn a lot of calories?" I asked.

"It depends on how fast and how long you run," Mom replied. "But in general, running is exercise, and exercise burns more calories than if you were sitting at home."

I shook my head. I couldn't believe it. I had been sabotaging myself by doing the thing that I loved almost every day. If running burned a lot of calories, then maybe I was accidentally making myself way too skinny.

That night I was able to fall asleep okay, but then I ended up having a nightmare. I was in a room piled high with donuts, and Jodie was timing me to see how long it would take me to eat them all.

She had a stopwatch and clicked it on as she told me, "If you can't do it in five minutes, then your legs will melt away!"

I gobbled down the donuts as quickly as I could, but there were hundreds and hundreds of them to eat. And I had no milk!

I felt like I had been eating donuts for hours, when Jodie clicked the stopwatch again.

"Too late!" she cackled.

I looked down. There were still dozens of uneaten donuts on the floor. But suddenly I was much closer to them than I had been just a second before.

With a sinking feeling, I realized that my legs were gone!

"Molly's got no legs, Molly can't play so-ccer," Jodie sang.

She sang that line over and over, her voice growing louder each time she repeated it until her words made all the uneaten donuts come crashing down, burying me.

I woke up in a sweat, my heart pounding. I sat up in bed and felt relief flood through me when I patted the covers and found my legs. I still had them.

But they were still too skinny.

I lay back down in bed. It took me a long time before I finally fell asleep.

Chapter Seven
The Worst Practice

Tuesday morning arrived, and all I wanted to do was stay in bed. I thought about going for a run, but it seemed like it was the hardest thing to do, even though it was a bright clear day, and the temperature was perfect for being outdoors.

When I had snoozed my alarm clock for the third time and couldn't delay any longer, I finally dragged myself out of bed and got ready for school.

"Want some breakfast?" Dad asked when I trudged downstairs and to the kitchen.

He was whisking eggs in a metal bowl, with the egg carton next to him. Next to him was a mug of coffee.

"Sure."

I breathed in the comforting scents. I don't like how bitter coffee tastes, but I do like the way it smells.

Dad cracked two more eggs into the bowl and stirred them up. Then he tipped the contents into a frying pan and began to cook the eggs over the stove with a wooden spatula.

"Sleep okay, Molly?" he asked as he worked on our breakfast.

"Not really." I dropped on the stool at the breakfast bar next to him and rubbed my eyes. "I had a bad dream, and it kept me up all night."

Dad took out two plates. He scraped the eggs onto them and put the frying pan in the sink.

"What was it about?" he asked as he got ketchup out of the fridge.

Out of all my family members, I feel like I can confide in my dad the most. But even though we're really close, I hesitated.

Dad is great when I'm working through my feelings about Kelsey, or Jenna, or being adopted as a baby, but I'd never had a conversation with him that had to do with the way I felt about my body.

"It's kind of personal and uncomfortable," I told him. "But I'll tell you if you want."

"That's what I'm here for." Dad passed me the ketchup and poured me a glass of orange juice while I squirted a long, red squiggly line over my eggs.

As we sat and ate, I told him about my nightmare. Then came the hard part. Dad, of course, wanted to know who Jodie was. I had to relive her words to me in the mall and at the clothing drive all over again when I told him about it.

It wasn't fun at all, but somehow I felt a little bit better now that Dad knew what was bothering me.

When I was done explaining, he took a sip of coffee from his mug, then set it down.

"Was the Jodie in your dream Jodie Perkins?"

I nodded, surprised. "How did you know?"

"I went to college with her parents. I was mostly friends with Jodie's dad, Bobby, but I got to know her mom, Caroline, because they were dating at the time."

Dad looked at me, his eyes a lot more serious than usual. "She was the star soccer player on the team, but she broke her leg sliding into another player in the championship game my senior year. She never recovered from that."

"Wow. It's too bad that an injury kept her from

playing the game she was so good at," I said.

Dad shook his head. "It was more than that. Caroline was very aggressive on the field, and she got a reputation over the years for being vindictive."

"What does that mean?" I asked. I had never heard the word before. It sounded scary.

"Vindictive means that you like to take revenge on people for wrongs that you think they've done to you," Dad answered. "Caroline always thought the refs were unfair, and that the opposing team's players were out to get her. What's more, she thought she was the sole reason for all the team's victories."

I raised my eyebrows. "Even if she was the best player in the world, that wouldn't be true."

I thought I was a pretty good player, but I still knew that a team doesn't win because of one person. A team wins because everyone is able to play well together and support one another. Coach Wendy had taught me that.

Dad nodded. "I agree. Caroline was the striker on the team. She was the one scoring most of the goals during the game, but she couldn't see that it was because her teammates were doing a great job of passing to her to score, or defending the goal really well when the ball got on the other half of the field."

I nodded, scooping the last bit of scrambled egg into my mouth.

"Just because you score a lot doesn't mean that you're the reason your team wins." I swallowed. "But I guess I feel kind of bad for her. Losing out on going professional because of any injury has got to be hard."

Dad took my empty plate and loaded it in the dishwasher along with his.

"It wasn't just that she broke her leg during that game. She had broken it deliberately trying to hurt a woman on the other team who she thought had tried to injure her in the last game they played against one another."

"Wow." I couldn't imagine resenting another player enough to want to hurt her. "Did she end up getting a red card?"

A red card in soccer is when the ref thinks that you've done something so bad that you get ejected from the game. Not only does the player have to leave the field and is banned from playing for the rest of the match, but they also can't have a substitute play for them, which means that the team is down a person for however long the game is played.

"She did," Dad said. "And the team eventually lost the championship. Even though Caroline eventually recovered, she couldn't run away from the fact that no professional sports team would sign on a player who was willing to hurt other people because of a perceived slight."

"I guess I wouldn't want to play with someone who was that awful to the other players."

I thought back to the night at the Park when Jodie's mom had been mean and snobby. I guess she still had a chip on her shoulder.

Dad looked at the clock. "Time for you to get to school," he said.

He came over and gave me a hug. "Don't let Jodie's words get to you. You are my strong, wonderful, amazing soccer star."

"Thanks, Dad."

I hugged him back, then grabbed my phone and backpack and yelled to Kelsey to hurry up so we could get to school on time.

School was okay, but kind of boring. I just barely got through my classes, floating through them as though they were nothing but things to pass the time before the big game.

Instead of raising my hand and answering questions like I usually did, I kept my head down and tried to concentrate on anything other than this weekend.

After school, I went for a run. I thought it would help me clear my head, but instead I spent the whole time worrying what my legs looked like to everyone I passed. Even with my leggings and shorts, they felt like they were on display for everyone to see.

When I got home, I checked my watch. The route that I had run was two miles. I had done it in nineteen minutes—one of my slowest times yet.

I wanted to cry. Running was the thing that grounded me. It was what made me feel good about myself, and pushing to get faster and faster times had always been a goal that I enjoyed working to achieve.

Now it looked like I was getting a lot worse. Instead of being the thing that kept me confident and happy, it was another way of realizing that I was in a body that could fail me. A body that was too skinny to be much of anything.

※　※　※　※　※

School on Wednesday came and went, and before I knew it, it was time for soccer practice. I raced to my locker and grabbed my soccer duffel, then threw on my uniform and headed toward the weight room off the gymnasium instead of outside. I still had twenty minutes before Coach Wendy took attendance, and I was going to make the most of it.

When I got inside, no one was there. I breathed a sigh of relief.

The top of my uniform was a loose jersey that made my body kind of shapeless, which was fine, but I only had soccer shorts to wear instead of pants. Even with my knee-high socks, I couldn't cover up my whole legs. I didn't want anyone watching while I did leg-strengthening exercises.

I did a series of squats and lunges, then sat against the wall at a ninety-degree angle until my muscles felt like they were burning up. Then I climbed on a leg-press machine and did a couple of reps, working my calves and quads.

When I was done, my legs were aching.

Good. Maybe they were beginning to get bigger.

I checked my phone and yelped. I had two minutes before soccer practice started. I grabbed my stuff and bolted from the weight room and ran out the back school exit.

When I arrived on the soccer field, all the girls were already there.

"Molly!" Coach Wendy raised her eyebrows. "You're three minutes late."

"I know, I know, I'm sorry," I said, panting. "I lost track of time."

Coach Wendy didn't say anything further, but I felt bad. I never lose track of time. Plus, this was our last practice before the big game against the Tigers on Sunday. And already it had gotten off to a rough start.

As we warmed up, I glanced over to my other teammates.

For the first time ever, I started comparing myself to them. Maddy is nearly as tall as I am, but she probably weighs a little bit more. She plays center back defense and is good at getting other players to pause by running toward them, then backing off at the last second.

I thought about all the times Maddy had outmaneuvered our opponents in a game. She would surprise them with her agility, which was a huge strength for our team.

Isabella is a little bit taller than Maddy and is super flexible. I've seen her do near splits when trying to get the ball, and her reach is always a little longer than everyone else's.

Riley is built like Jodie—small and sturdy. Even though she's shorter than I am, she can move just as fast.

As I looked over everyone, I realized that I had always been proud of my slender figure. But maybe looking slender gave the impression that I was weak and scrawny.

Maybe when Annie, Coach Wendy's sister, came to our game, she would take one look at me and dismiss me. Maybe she would think, how could a star college soccer champion come from such a skinny body?

"Molly? Earth to Molly!" Coach Wendy's voice broke through my thoughts.

I looked up and realized that warm-ups were over and the rest of the girls had gathered on one side of the field for drills. I was the only one left standing in our warm-up area.

"Sorry," I said, for the second time. I ran over and joined my teammates.

"Hey, are you okay?" Maddy asked me. Her face was a mask of worry.

"Do you think I look too thin?" I asked her.

Maddy groaned, then covered her mouth. "I'm sorry. I didn't mean to do that." She crossed her arms. "Are you still thinking about what Jodie said to you?"

"OMG, there's so much more!" I realized that Maddy only knew what Jodie had said at the mall. I quickly filled her in about being made fun of for my skinny legs at the clothing drive.

"I can't believe her!" Maddy opened her mouth to say more, but then drills started and we had to concentrate.

During our running drills, for the first time I was the slowest member on the team during our sprints. I tried to get my legs to go faster, but they felt like lead.

Of course, it probably didn't help that I had worked out in the weight room right before practice. Still, I felt slow and clumsy.

When it came time to do dribbling skills and pass the ball between a tight set of cones, I couldn't seem to get my feet to work right. I kept dribbling too long or too short.

Then we practiced our passing skills. For this round, Isabella got paired up with Riley, so it was just Maddy and me passing the ball to one another.

After my fifth time kicking the ball way wide to her, Maddy finally put her foot on top of the ball, trapping it in place.

"Molly, you've really got to concentrate," she said. "This will be our last chance to practice our passing before the game on Sunday."

"I know! I'm trying," I replied. But it was really hard to keep track of where the ball was when I kept comparing my legs to all the girls around me.

The last drill we had was three-on-three scrimmages. Maddy, Isabella, and I were on a team, while Sara and Addie, two of our defenders, and Riley were on another.

We faced off against one another, and Coach Wendy blew her whistle. I was in the center and managed to take control of the ball. As I was running downfield, Riley intercepted me. I tried to fake left and go right, but she was a step ahead of me and tapped the ball right out from under my foot.

We both lunged to take control of it, but Riley got there first. She pivoted, and then passed the ball to Sara, who ran it toward our goal. Maddy headed toward her and managed to steal the ball away just as Sara was about to kick it into the goal.

I ran hard downfield and managed to get about twenty yards away from Riley, who was guarding me. I was wide open!

Maddy saw me and aimed a long kick in my direction. I saw the ball hurtling down the field, perfectly aimed toward me. It landed against my foot with a satisfying thunk.

I dribbled the ball toward the goal, concentrating on getting it near enough to shoot. Just as I got to the penalty area, Riley appeared next to me. She got ahead of me and turned around, blocking my shot on goal.

I dribbled right. Riley went right.

I dribbled left. Riley was right there with me.

I wasn't going to get a clear shot on goal. I had to pass the ball. I saw Maddy across the field, running hard to assist.

I rolled the ball back, swung around, and was about to pass to Maddy when Riley jumped to stop me. Suddenly, all I saw was how gracefully she moved, and how different her body type was from mine.

She was the perfect soccer player. And I was not.

Distracted, I stopped. It gave Riley a chance to take the ball, but before she could, I saw her coming and snapped out of it. Frantically I kicked the ball, but it was way too hard. The ball sailed past Maddy and over the sideline.

"Out of bounds!" Coach Wendy called. "Play goes to Riley, Sara, and Addy."

Riley kicked the ball from the sidelines, and it went straight toward Addy, who dribbled the ball past Isabella and took a shot on goal.

The ball flew through the air and landed against the net. It was a perfect goal for the other team.

The rest of the scrimmage went the same way. I just couldn't get my act together, and by the time we were done, my team hadn't scored one goal, while Riley's team had scored nine.

"Great work today," Coach Wendy told us as practice ended. "I think we're in terrific shape to play against the Tigers this weekend."

Coach was being encouraging, but her words sounded hollow to my ears. I hadn't done great work today. In fact, I had been pretty lousy.

It was not the best way to end the last practice before Coach Wendy's sister was going to show up to the game.

As we got changed, all I could think about

was how sad and small and wimpy my legs looked compared to everyone else.

I didn't deserve to be the star player of the Falcons. Not with my performance at practice. And not with this thin, gangly body that just didn't seem to want to do anything right.

Chapter Eight
Don't Have to Prove Anything

I was sitting in my room after school the next day, trying to do my homework, when I heard a knock at the door.

"Time to go!" Mom peeked her head in with a big smile.

"Go to what?" I asked.

"The clothing drive!" Mom frowned. "You didn't forget, did you?"

I put a hand over my face. I had completely forgotten about telling Mom that I would sort clothes another day because we had been at the drive for so little time on Sunday. "Mom, do I have to go? I'm really busy with homework."

Mom's head drooped just a little. "Sure, honey,"

she said. "I'll give Ms. Castro a call and let her know that you're not coming."

"Wait . . . why do you have to let her know? I thought this was an event where people just dropped by," I said.

"Well, Sunday was like that because the library anticipated there would be a lot of interested volunteers on a weekend. But a weekday—Thursday—is a lot trickier because people don't necessarily have time in their work schedules to volunteer."

Mom pulled out her phone. "Ms. Castro called me last night asking if you and I could come again. A huge donation of boxes came in, and she was worried that it would take a long time to sort it, since she wasn't sure there would be any volunteers tonight. I told her that we would both be there."

I didn't want to go back to the library. I didn't want to have to relive what Jodie had said to me, or how she had made me feel.

But the library was doing a great thing by helping out the community with the clothing drive. And now it really could use some extra hands.

I decided that it was more important to volunteer for a cause that needed help than to worry about how the common room in the library would make me feel.

I visit the library a lot, so at some point, I'd have to get over any fears of running into Jodie there. Plus, the chances of Jodie being there with her mom were pretty slim. I was sure she was doing something all professional and soccer-related three days before our big game.

"Don't call Ms. Castro," I said, closing my math textbook. "I'm coming."

"What about your homework?" Mom asked.

"I'll do it in the car." I put my textbook and sheet of homework in my backpack, then stood up. "I'm ready."

"That's my girl!" Mom put her phone away, and together we headed down the stairs. "I'm proud of you for volunteering twice this week, even though Jazz Fest and your game against the Tigers are both coming up this weekend. It's a lot to think about."

"Well, maybe volunteering will help me get my mind off things. After all I do like organizing stuff."

I tried to sound enthusiastic, even though there was a sinking feeling in the pit of my stomach.

We drove to the library, where we met Ms. Castro

at the common-room entrance. While she said hello to my mom, I peeked inside. There were about twenty huge boxes that still had to be opened and sorted.

There were only three sorting tables set up, and I saw only two volunteers, stacking enormous piles of clothes on top of one another. None of the volunteers were Jodie or her mom.

Whew.

"Molly, it's so good to see you again!" Ms. Castro said. "Your mother was such a sweetheart when I called her and said that we needed help today. We got an incredible donation—someone with eight children who are all grown now was going through the years of clothes that they had collected and decided to give them all away. Which is wonderful news, but a lot of work for us. Thank you for coming."

"You're welcome," I said, smiling up at Ms. Castro. When I saw how happy she was to see Mom and me, I felt a jolt of happiness too.

Sometimes it was just good to forget everything about life and help others out.

Mom and I headed toward the one table that wasn't being used and began to sort through boxes.

I folded pants and sweaters, loads of long-sleeved

T-shirts, fuzzy wool hats, mittens, gloves. In every box there were a bunch of mismatched socks that I sorted patiently through, matching them pair by pair. It was strangely satisfying.

We volunteers had gone through about half the boxes when Ms. Castro came in holding one side of another folding table for sorting.

On the other side of the folding table was Jodie's mom.

I froze, my hands instinctively bunching up against a sweaterdress that I had just taken from one of the boxes.

I looked for a way to make an exit before Jodie could see me, but there wasn't really anywhere I could go. Because there were so few people in the room, I couldn't duck behind someone.

I ducked under the table instead. It was a silly move, but it was the only thing I could think of doing.

"Molly? What are you doing?" Mom asked, staring down at me in confusion.

"I . . . uh . . . dropped a sock. I'm looking for it now," I replied lamely.

I pretended to hunt under the table for a long time, silently hoping that Jodie and her mom would not be there for too long. But when I stood up, I came face-to-face with Jodie.

She was standing right in front of my table. Her mom was across the room, opening a box to sort.

"Hey, Molly," Jodie said. She ran a hand through her short hair. "Can I talk to you for a second?"

I wanted to say no and dash out of there, but there was something in Jodie's expression that made me stop. She looked like she wasn't going to attack me or say something rude.

In fact, she looked a little sheepish.

"Um, sure?" I said.

Jodie quickly glanced at my mom, and then back at me. "Molly, would you be okay if we went for a walk around the library and talked? I kind of want us to have a little bit of private time."

I looked at Mom, and she nodded. "Sure, Molly, go ahead. I'll be here for the next hour at least."

I shoved my hands in my pockets and followed Jodie upstairs and out the door. She was silent as we walked past the parking lot, and to a small gravel lane that wound around the library.

When no one was near, Jodie took a deep breath and spoke up.

"Molly, this has really been bugging me. I was out of line with my comments the other day. I'm sorry. I shouldn't have made fun of you at the mall. And I'm sorry about the crack I made about your legs at the clothing drive last Sunday. I'm pretty self-conscious about my body, and I know that when someone says something like that to you, it really sticks in your head."

"It did," I told her. "I can't stop thinking about how skinny I am. Or how my body isn't really great for soccer. I keep comparing myself to the other girls on the team, when I didn't used to before."

I sighed. "And I keep comparing myself to you. Your mom is famous for being a great soccer player, and you've inherited her physique, which is so different from mine."

Jodie laughed. It startled me, because I didn't know why what I said was so funny.

"I didn't inherit her physique," Jodie said. "I'm adopted."

At first what Jodie said was so surprising, I couldn't process it. "You're . . . what?" I asked.

Now it was Jodie's turn to sigh. "I was given up by my birth mother when I was three because she couldn't take care of me anymore, and I ended up being adopted by the Perkins family about nine years ago. I know my mom and I look a lot alike, but we're not related at all."

"Wow." Everything that I had thought about Jodie was crashing down on me. "So, the fact that your mom was good at soccer isn't why you're good?"

"I'm good because she's put a lot of pressure on me to follow in her footsteps," said Jodie. "I really have been playing soccer since I was three."

Her face fell. "Mom says winning is my only option, and she pushes that on me all the time. I guess I'm just overly competitive because of that. Sometimes I wish I were less competitive."

"I can be competitive too," I said to Jodie. "Coach Wendy says that as long as the team works together, she doesn't care about winning. But I care about winning a lot. Maybe sometimes more than the rest of the team."

I took a deep breath. I wanted to tell Jodie that I understood where she was coming from.

"I'm adopted too," I said. "You probably know that because I don't look anything like my mom."

Jodie nodded.

"And part of being adopted means wondering if you have to work extra hard to belong to a family," I added.

"Yeah, I feel exactly like that!" Jodie chimed in. "I think I push myself because sometimes I feel that being adopted means I have to prove myself all the time. That I deserve love."

"Here's the thing," I said. "Being adopted means that your family really, really, *really* wants you. It means that they chose you out of all the kids that they could have adopted because they thought you would make their family bigger and better. Being adopted means that from the very beginning, your adoptive family wanted you."

Jodie stopped walking and stood still for a long moment.

"I never thought about it that way," she said slowly.

"You don't have to prove anything to anyone just because you're adopted," I told her. "My mom and dad have often said to me that the best thing I can do is just to be open and curious about the world, and to find activities that I find interesting and care about and pursue them. Like soccer."

I paused. "Honestly, they wouldn't mind if I was

the worst soccer player on the team. They would still encourage me because they'd know I was doing something I loved."

"You know, you're right." Jodie looked back toward the library. "I think my mom is trying to relive her soccer-star days. She's on my case constantly to eat, breathe, and sleep soccer. But my dad's not like that. He's just happy that I'm doing something I really like."

She giggled. "Want to hear a secret?"

"Sure," I said. We had circled around the library and were walking down to the common-room entrance.

"I actually want to be a tennis player when I grow up. I tried it out this summer and really liked it." She looked down at her legs. "Even though I don't have the body for it."

"Now don't you go being self-conscious about your body!" I said, laughing but shaking my head at the same time. "You've done enough damage by making me nervous about the way I look."

Jodie's face turned serious. "Molly, I'm really sorry that I made you feel that way. I don't know if you know this, but your dad called my dad to tell him about what happened between the two of us, and my dad talked to me about how bad it is to criticize someone's body. It's mean to say to anybody, but especially someone who's competitive and plays sports."

So that's why Jodie was apologizing!

I felt a tidal wave of love for my dad, who had listened to me talk and had done something about it. Sometimes, having a parent step in can be a good thing.

"Apology accepted," I told Jodie.

"You know, I think I said all those words because I was kind of intimidated by you," Jodie said. "I've always thought that tall and thin was the way that the best soccer players looked."

"Well, I thought that small and muscular was the perfect body type for soccer," I said.

"Maybe it's both," Jodie replied. "Maybe all kinds of bodies can play soccer, and be good at it."

"It just depends on how much you practice. And how much you love the sport," I added.

We had reached the entrance to the library. Before we went in, Jodie stuck out her hand.

"We're okay?" she asked.

I took her hand in mine. "We're more than okay," I said firmly. "We're great."

We went inside, and each of us found our moms. We helped finish sorting all the donations and got a dozen thank-yous from Ms. Castro before we headed to our cars to go home.

I didn't talk much while I watched the road go by, but my heart felt lighter than it had been for the past week. There was so much anxiety and self-criticism that had been building in me, and it turned out that I shouldn't have worried.

Jodie thought I looked great.

And even if she didn't, it didn't matter. I was responsible for how I felt about my body, not anyone else. And right about now, I could feel my limbs, long and slender, stretching and eager to run.

That night before the sun went down, I went out with my running shorts and sneakers tied just right. It was warmer than it had been in previous days, so I was only wearing a T-shirt, too.

As I raced through the neighborhood, I felt strength flowing through my muscles as the blood pumped through them. My bare knees and calves flashed by streets and corners, past neighbors turning to wave hello or to shout words of encouragement as I passed by.

I no longer felt like I had to hide my legs.

Now they were symbols of pride, and of the work I had done, year after year, through running and soccer, to make them sure and powerful while playing the game that I loved so much.

Chapter Nine
Jazz Fest

The next night was Family Fest. For the first time all week, I actually really relaxed with my family and had a good time with Mom, Kelsey, Jenna, and my cousin Lindsay.

As usual, we went to Louie Louie to gorge on fried ravioli and slices of ooey, gooey butter cake, and laughed and chatted the whole time, talking about how excited we were go help out with Jazz Fest—even if it did mean waking up extra early the next morning.

Grandpa's ambitious idea of giving away two hundred donuts meant that we had to decorate and box two hundred donuts super early in the morning, since donuts that are over a day old can go stale.

Grandpa prided himself on waking up at three a.m. so that he could roll and fry the donut dough and have the donuts fresh for the day. He only served donuts that were made the day he sold them. The rest we would donate to the local food pantry.

When Mom, Jenna, Kelsey, and I arrived at the Park at five in the morning, Grandpa was just finishing up with frying the donuts.

In the quiet morning light he ushered us into the empty dining room and toward a large table at the back of the restaurant. Hundreds of plain donuts in bins were waiting for us, along with tubs of toppings.

Before we started, Grandpa let us each decorate a donut that we also got to eat. Jenna went for a spicy apple cider donut, while Kelsey chose cinnamon crunch. Mom opted for a hint of vanilla one.

I chose the hot cocoa flavor, rolling the donut in chocolate powder until it was completely covered. I then drizzled a little bit of marshmallow icing on top for the final touch. It looked beautiful.

"Here," Grandpa said, handing each of us a glass of milk.

He raised his own glass high. "I'd like to make a toast," he said.

"Go, Grandpa!" Kelsey cheered, while the rest of us giggled.

I really love being with my family. It felt so comfortable to be around this table, and part of a business that celebrates food and laughter and love.

"I'd like to say thank you to all of you who make the Park and Jazz Fest so special," Grandpa began. "When Nans and I started the restaurant, we didn't know if we were going to succeed. All we knew was that we had each other."

He looked at each of us and smiled. "Now we still have each other, and so much more! This restaurant keeps the bills paid, but it also keeps our family together. I can't say how proud I am of all of you, and the work that you do to make this place special."

"Well, I want to thank you, Grandpa, for having the courage to pursue your dream and do what you love," Mom said. "You and Nans are inspiring to all your children, and your grandchildren, too!"

"I like to think that Nans and I are always doing our best." Grandpa nodded. "We're always thinking about how to make the restaurant better, how to make our food the most delicious it can be, how to experiment and try new things to keep ourselves fresh and on our toes, and how to make sure that generations of our family want to come back to the restaurant to be part of our legacy."

Grandpa smiled at Jenna, Kelsey, and me. "And that goes for all you grandchildren, too. I see you doing your best in everything you do, whether it be school or sports or helping out at the Park. I know I'm supposed to be the wise old teacher, but honestly, *you* inspire *me*."

I felt tears welling up in my eyes, but they were the good kind, the kind that made you feel like you were part of a really magical moment. I was so happy to be adopted into a family that loved so openly and was always there to help one another be the best they could be.

As we sat at the table and ate our donuts, I looked around and realized that my family was just like my soccer team. We were all part of a group striving to always be better, while listening to one another and making sure that everyone felt like they belonged.

All week long I had been worrying about Coach Wendy's sister scrutinizing my every play, looking at me and only me while I was out on the field. Now I realized that I didn't have to care about that. I would give it my all at the big game tomorrow and not worry about anything except playing as well as I could with the awesome teammates that I had.

I didn't have to impress Coach Wendy's sister. I just had to have a good time.

I popped the last piece of hot cocoa donut into my mouth. As the chocolatey, sugary, donutty flavor swirled around my mouth, I felt a happiness that came from eating something delicious, but also being part of the process that made it delicious.

I swallowed my donut bite down with the last of my milk, then got to work. Besides the two hundred donuts we were donating, we still had to box up tons of donuts to sell.

Jenna and I squirted all sorts of different new fillings into donuts—jams, flavored creams, and caramel—and applied frostings to their tops.

Kelsey, who was the most artistic of all of us, decorated the donuts. She would add a dash of sprinkles or pipe out icing designs like music notes in bright colors or saxophones.

When we were done decorating the donuts, Mom and Lily and Lindsay's best friend Casey (who sometimes helped out at the Park) packed the ones that we were giving away to customers into individual boxes. Mom wrote on each box in her curly, delicate handwriting what flavor each donut was, to make sure the customer knew what he or she was getting.

It took a couple of hours, but when we had finished, in addition to the hundreds of donuts that we were selling at our booth on Main Street for Jazz Fest, we also had two hundred boxes of donuts ready for Grandpa's grand giveaway.

We were tired, but very proud of ourselves.

As we were sweeping up and washing the now-empty tubs, Uncle Mike and Uncle Charlie came into the kitchen. Uncle Mike runs Donut Dreams, while Uncle Charlie orders all our supplies and makes sure that everything is stocked and nothing runs out. Together they make a pretty great team.

Today, though, instead of working at the donut counter, they were going to be selling donuts at the booth we had set up along Main Street. One of the best parts about our town festivals is that all the food vendors that show up.

A lot of them are like us—restaurants that take their best-selling items and sell them from booths lined up along the street—but there are some vendors from out of town who specialize in festival food, like pretzels, fried dough, popcorn, roasted corn, and deep-fried onion rings.

I always loved getting a hot drink at Jazz Fest especially if it was extra cold outside. There was a stand that sold hot cocoa and hot cider, and it was always a struggle to decide which one to choose.

As Uncle Mike and Uncle Charlie began loading the donuts into a van to drive to Main Street, Mom looked at her phone.

"The Jazz Fest parade starts in half an hour. Want to go watch it?"

"Yes!" Kelsey, Jenna, and I all shouted. We had done our part to help out with Jazz Fest. Now it was time to enjoy it!

We raced into the car and drove to the center of town. It was a little hard finding parking because everyone was there, but Mom found the last free spot in the parking lot across the street from the library.

We got to Main Street just in time to hear the high school band start the official Jazz Fest parade. There were trumpets, trombones, a few tubas, and a drum, along with clarinets, saxophones, and flutes. Everyone was wearing our town's school colors.

The marching band was followed by a whole line of amazing floats that different groups had put together over the past couple of weeks. The fire department had made a giant papier-mâché float of their Dalmatian fire dog, Nellie, who sat on top of it and barked and grinned at the crowd.

The rotary club followed them with a massive turkey float, and there were many high school floats, which looked a lot less detailed, but you could see that everyone on the floats was super proud of the fact that they had made them.

It was a great beginning to an even more awesome day. After the parade was over, Mom, Kelsey, Jenna, and I went to the town square, where we listened to a bunch of bands play music.

Then we got lunch at one of the booths along Main Street that sold these delicious savory pastries that they called shepherd's pie pockets. They were like calzones, only instead of red sauce and cheese, there was ground beef, mashed potatoes, and peas.

After eating lunch, it was time for midday dessert!

We stopped by the Donut Dreams booth to see how everything was going, and had to wait for ten minutes because the line was so long.

Normally I get a little impatient waiting for food, but this time I didn't mind at all. A long wait meant that the booth was doing really well.

When we finally got up front, Uncle Mike greeted us with a smile.

"How's business, Mike?" Mom asked him.

"Even better than last year!" Uncle Mike replied.

He pointed to a sign that said, GET A FREE DONUT WITH EVERY PURCHASE WHILE SUPPLIES LAST!

"This promotion that Grandpa came up with is really working. I've had so many orders for five donuts, when usually people only ask for one or two."

"Are there any of Grandpa's new flavors that seem to be the most popular?" Jenna asked.

Uncle Mike nodded. "Hot cocoa, by far. It's only one o'clock, and we've already run out of them!"

I smiled. It was nice to hear that my favorite new flavor seemed to be the town's favorite new flavor too!

"Well, we don't want to be holding up the line," Mom said. "Girls, what do you want?"

Jenna ordered an apple pie donut, while Kelsey opted for a chocolate glazed donut with rainbow sprinkles.

When it was my turn to order, I was about to ask for a plain old-fashioned, when Uncle Mike reached under the table and pulled out a hot cocoa donut.

"I thought you ran out!" I gasped.

Uncle Mike smiled. "We did. But your mom told me that this was your favorite kind, so I saved one for you. Here you go," he said, handing me the powdery, chocolatey dessert of amazingness.

Mom paid for the donuts (even though it was a family business and the money technically went back to all of us, she still liked to support the booth).

"See you at the bonfire tonight!" she called to Uncle Mike and Uncle Charlie as we scooted out of line to let other customers order.

"Looking forward to it!" Uncle Mike called back. "Save some s'mores for me!"

When Jazz Fest is just about winding down, the town lights a gigantic bonfire by the lake. The whole town gathers around it to get cozy and roast marshmallows to make s'mores.

Then everyone brings chairs and blankets and lines them up along the lake to watch the fireworks that end the festival.

We spent most of the rest of the afternoon looking

at all the festival sights on Main Street. Then, when it was around four o'clock, my phone pinged. I took it out and smiled.

There was a message from Maddy waiting for me.

U ready to paint our nails?

I wrote back,

YEAH!!! When? Where?

4:30. Gazebo.

Isabella will be there too.

"Mom, can I meet up with Maddy and Isabella at the gazebo?" I asked.

The gazebo is in the center of the town square, right by the lake. It's where we would be heading as a family later anyway, on our way to the bonfire.

Mom nodded. "I'll pick you up from there around six," she said.

That gave me an hour and a half to paint my nails and talk about the game tomorrow with my friends.

It was perfect. I ran to the end of Main Street and toward the town square. I saw Maddy and Isabella waiting for me there.

"Molly! Over here!" Maddy waved her hand in my direction.

I joined them on a blanket that Isabella had set up on the grass. All three of us pulled out our sparkly red nail polish.

Maddy dug into her bag and held up Q-tips and nail polish remover. "Just in case there's an accident," she said.

As we sat and took out our bottles of nail polish, Isabella's phone chimed. She took it out of her pocket and glanced at it.

"Yes!" she cheered. "Riley just said she was in for wearing the polish to our big game. She was the last person on the team who hadn't responded. That means tomorrow when we face off against the Tigers, we're all going to have the coolest matching fingers!"

"That's awesome!" I said. "I love how we're all going into this together."

Maddy glanced at me as she opened her bottle of polish. "Are you nervous about seeing Jodie on the field?" she asked me.

I palmed my hand against my face.

"I completely forgot to tell you!" I quickly filled her and Isabella in on the conversation we'd had at the library.

"We're all cool now," I said. "And when we play each other, I think it's going to be exciting and competitive—but also a lot of fun."

Maddy hugged me. "That's so great to hear, Molly!"

"I can't believe she's adopted!" Isabella said as she applied the bright red polish to her thumb. "She looks so much like Mrs. Perkins."

"I thought so too," I said. I had finished painting my left hand and held it up to admire it. "But you know what? It was really good to bond with her about being adopted. Both of us thought we had something prove, when really all we have to do is love what we do and have our families support us."

"That sounds like a great way to think about it!" Maddy held her bottle of polish out to me. "I can never paint my right hand—my left hand gets all shaky and my nails end up sloppy. Will you do it?"

"Of course!"

I took the bottle and carefully painted Maddy's

right hand, then had Isabella paint my right hand.

Finally, Maddy painted Isabella's left hand (Isabella is left-handed), so by the end, everyone's nails were painted. We had done such a good job, we didn't even have to use the Q-tips or nail polish remover!

As the sun began to set, we held our hands up and waved them around to let our nails dry. When they were done, they were smooth and shiny and beautifully colored.

"Molly, time to head to the bonfire!"

I turned my head and saw Mom walking toward me, with Jenna and Kelsey right behind her.

"Coming!" I stood up and gestured toward Maddy and Isabella. "Want to go down to the lake with me?"

"We told Maddy's mom that we would wait for her here," said Isabella. "But she should be coming soon. We'll text when we get there and come find you."

I joined Mom and my sisters and together we met our whole extended family by the lake. There was my dad, Grandpa, Nans, my uncle Mike and my uncle Charlie, and my cousins Lindsay, Skylar, Rich, and Lily.

We spread two huge blankets on the ground, and everyone sat and ate s'mores as we waited for the fireworks to start. I got to sit next to Grandpa, who looked tired but very happy.

"How did your Jazz Fest giveaway go?" I asked him.

"It was incredible," Grandpa replied. "Not only did we sell out of donuts, but we also ran out of all the new donut flavors that I was giving away." He sighed happily. "It's a dream come true."

"Well, you worked hard for your dream—you deserve for it to come true," I told him.

Just then fireworks exploded into the sky. I leaned my head against Grandpa's shoulder and felt the happiness of the day wash over me.

Regardless of what happened at the game tomorrow, everything was going to be okay.

Chapter Ten
The Big Game

The next morning I woke up feeling excited. I got dressed and ran downstairs, where Dad was in the kitchen, stirring a pot of oatmeal.

"Breakfast is almost ready," he told me. "I thought you might like something special before your big game this afternoon."

"What makes it special?" I glanced at the pot. It seemed to be just plain oatmeal to me.

"The toppings!" Dad replied.

He ladled some oatmeal into a bowl, then added sliced bananas, pumpkin seeds, and fresh blueberries from the fridge. He topped it off with a drizzle of maple syrup, then served it to me with a tall glass of orange juice.

"Thanks, Dad," I said, digging in with a spoon.

It was one of the best breakfasts I had ever eaten!

"How are you feeling?" Dad asked me as he sat down to enjoy his own bowl of fancy oatmeal.

I grinned. "Good. This whole week has been a roller coaster, but the last couple of days have been great. Jazz Fest was so much fun!"

I took a swig of orange juice and gulped it down. "And I'm really glad Jodie and I were able to talk on Thursday and smooth things over. Before, I was dreading this game. Now I'm looking forward to it!"

"I can't wait to see you out on the field today," Dad said. "You're going to crush it!"

Suddenly I remembered the reason why Jodie and I had ended up talking. I put down my spoon and went over to my dad.

"Jodie told me that you called her dad and spoke with him. Thanks for doing that," I said, giving him a quiet hug.

Dad gave me a fierce hug back. "That's what parents are supposed to do."

He lifted his head suddenly.

"Oh! I spoke with Kelsey and Jenna this morning. They know that this is an important game for you, so we'll all be there—me, Mom, and your sisters."

My heart got so big, I thought it was going to explode with happiness. This afternoon my family would be there to support me. And that was all that mattered.

❊ ❊ ❊ ❊ ❊

A few hours later, it was time to get ready. I packed my cleats and water bottle, then changed into my uniform. As I was rolling my long knee-high socks up and over my calves, I looked down at my legs. They weren't too long or too skinny. They were just right.

Dad drove us all to the soccer field. When we arrived, my family made their way to the bleachers while I walked over to the end of the field, where the Falcons were warming up by our goal.

Coach Wendy was there as well, talking to a woman who looked almost exactly like her. When Coach Wendy saw me, she waved me over.

"Molly! I'd like you to meet my sister Annie," she said.

"It's nice to meet you," I said, shaking Annie's hand.

"Same here," Annie replied. "Wendy has been

telling me a lot about you. I'm looking forward to seeing you out on the field!"

If I had met Annie a week ago, I think I would have been so overwhelmed by stress, I wouldn't have been able to talk to her.

Now, I felt strong and confident and sure.

"Well, I'm going to do my best out there," I said. "And I know everyone else will be giving it their all too. As Coach Wendy says, it's not about winning or losing, it's working together as a team."

"And that's why she's a great coach," Annie said, smiling warmly at her sister. "People sometimes think that star players are what make a team special. They are important, but what's more important is how the team plays as a group. You could have the best striker in the world, but they aren't going to carry you to a championship if you don't have a strong second striker and hardworking midfielders to pass them the ball, or great defense players."

Coach Wendy nodded, then looked at her watch. "Kickoff is in five," she called to the team. "Group huddle!"

I ran over to the rest of my team and we gathered in a tight circle.

"Everyone in," Coach Wendy said.

We all put our hands on top of one another in the center of the circle. It was as if the fireworks from Jazz Fest last night were reflected in our nails—red, shiny, and sparkling.

"One, two . . . three!" Coach Wendy yelled.

"Gooooooooo, Falcons!" we yelled in unison, lifting our hands high.

We broke from the huddle and the eleven of us who were starting jogged out to each of our positions.

Maddy, Riley, and I played offense, so we were in the center circle area in the very middle of the field.

The Tigers' offense was there as well. I saw Jodie coming toward us, her short blond hair glinting in the sun. She looked tough and determined.

"You look ready to play," I told her.

"You do too." Jodie grinned. "May the best team win."

The coaches and ref came over to start the game. The ref tossed a coin in the air while Coach Wendy called heads.

The coin landed in the ref's outstretched palm, and he quickly slapped it over the top of his other hand.

"Heads it is!" he said.

Since Coach Wendy had called heads, she got to say whether we would have control of the ball first, or at the beginning of the second half of the game.

But instead of choosing, Coach Wendy turned to us. "What would you girls like to do?" she asked.

I looked at my teammates. "Want to take the kickoff now?" I asked them.

Everyone nodded in unison.

The coaches walked off the field, and the ref held up a stopwatch. He blew a whistle, and the game was on!

I passed the ball forward to Maddy, who tapped it back to me. I dribbled down the field, dodged past Jodie, and then made a clean pass to Riley.

Riley ran down the field with the ball and made it to the penalty box before the Tigers' center back kicked the ball away from her and toward Jodie, who ran the ball all the way past the midfield.

As offense, we hung back and watched as our defense took over.

Isabella tried to block Jodie with a sliding tackle, but Jodie moved around her like liquid, running and dribbling the ball, then passed to the Tigers' second striker. The second striker moved the ball to the penalty box, faked a shot on goal, but then passed to Jodie, who kicked the ball toward our goal.

Meghan, our goalie, dove for the ball, but it swished past her and into the net.

It was Tigers 1, Falcons 0.

I could have been disheartened, but instead of getting frustrated or sad, as I passed Jodie on the field I said, "Good work."

Jodie looked and me and smiled. "Thanks," she said.

Then she waved to her family in the stands, who were holding up a colorful sign saying, JODIE ROCKS!

I looked at the bleachers and saw my family sitting there, cheering me on.

"We love you, Molly!" they called.

I grinned and shouted, "I love you, too!" back at them.

Once again, I realized that even though Jodie and I were playing against one another, we had families who supported us no matter what.

I got possession of the ball and dribbled it down the field. Jodie got right in front of me to block any forward pass I might make, but I saw that Riley was open to my left, and instead of moving the ball forward, I sent it horizontally over to her.

Riley tapped the ball to stop it, then passed it back to Sara, who kicked it long to Maddy, who was way down the field. Maddy took a shot on goal, but the Tigers' goalkeeper snatched the ball right before it went past the goal line. She threw it to the center back, who passed it to a winger.

Before the winger could kick the ball, I ran next to her and tapped the ball out from her foot, gaining possession of it. I ran toward the penalty box, my heart thumping with adrenaline.

The Tigers' center back crouched low and angled toward me, jockeying to slow me down. I couldn't get a clean shot on goal, but I saw that Maddy was open.

I kicked the ball hard. It sailed over to Maddy, who, with perfect precision, headed the ball into the goal. It was 1–1!

"Good work," a voice said from behind me.

I turned around and grinned. "Thanks," I said to Jodie.

The rest of the game went by in a blizzard of dribbles, passes, tackles, and shots.

With a minute to spare, we were tied 7–7 and had time for only one last play. Jodie got the ball and dribbled it down the field. Maddy intercepted her and kicked the ball my way.

I dribbled it down the field and passed to Riley, who took her first shot on goal of the game.

It went in! As the scoreboard flipped to 8–7, the ref blew the whistle. The game was over, and we had won!

The Falcons came together in the center of the field, forming a laughing, yelling, happy pile. I hugged my teammates, and they hugged me back.

I had the best family, but I had the best soccer team too. In that moment everything felt just right.

"Attention!" Coach Wendy called.

We all stopped what we were doing and stood very still. We knew it was an important moment.

"Would the following players please come over. Molly, Maddy, Jodie, and Jocelyn." (The last name I didn't recognize—she must have been a Tigers player.)

We trotted over and stood in front of Coach Wendy. Annie was beside her, holding a clipboard and pen.

"Great game, everyone!" Annie declared. "I know

you're still in middle school, but I haven't seen teams work so well together in a long time. And you four were extremely talented out on the field."

I couldn't believe it. Annie thought that we were good soccer players! I was so proud of myself, and the other girls too.

"Was there anything in particular that we did well?" Jocelyn asked.

Annie nodded. "What I loved seeing about you all was how generous you were on the field. You are all strong players, but you gave other players chances to shine too. I'm always looking for players who are not only individually talented, but who instinctively understand that teamwork is far more important than being a star."

She held her clipboard out to Jocelyn. "After watching this game, I'd like to get all of your contact information."

I had an exciting hunch as to why Annie would ask for our phone numbers and e-mails, but I wanted to check just to make sure.

"Do you think any of us have a shot at going to college on a soccer scholarship?" I asked her.

Annie nodded. "With hard work and effort, I can

see you all having the potential to make it on a college soccer team. Maybe even on a full-ride scholarship."

I felt like I was floating. This had been such an incredible game, and it sounded like one of my biggest dreams could actually become reality, according to an actual soccer scout!

When Annie's clipboard came to me, I carefully printed my name, phone number, and e-mail on it.

As I went to join my family in the bleachers, I saw Jodie walking ahead of me to meet her family.

I ran to catch up with her.

"Jodie!" I called when I was close.

Jodie turned to me. "Hey, Molly. Good game today."

"Thanks. You did amazing," I said. "You were really a soccer star out there."

"You know, I was," Jodie said slowly and thoughtfully. "And you are too!"

She looked down at the ground. "At first I was intimidated by you because you were so good, but now I see there's room for more than one soccer star on the field. I like being challenged by you."

"Agreed," I said. "I've never worked harder in a game, and I think it was because you kept me on my toes the entire time. In order to outplay you, I had to think and push and make creative choices every single play. And you know what? It was awesome, and I learned a lot from you."

Jodie paused, then spoke. "You know, normally would be sulking because we lost the game, but I have to say—this game was really fun. We both played our best, and I'm proud of the work that I did out there today."

"You should be," I told her. "You're an amazing player. You've got a very different style of play than I'm used to, but it works for you."

"It does," Jodie replied with a grin. "And next time I see you on the field, I'm going to use my style and talent to win!"

I laughed. Jodie was still competitive, but there was a warmth and humor to her that softened her fighting words.

We had reached the bleachers. I said goodbye to Jodie, then ran up to my family.

"You did such a great job, honey!" Dad said. "I'm so proud of you."

"Was that the college soccer scout you were talking to?" Mom asked, tilting her head toward Annie.

"It was! She's going to keep in touch with me and Maddy and a few other girls in high school," I said. "She thinks we all have the potential to play college soccer!"

Jenna gave me a hug. "That's awesome, Molly. You deserve it."

"I say we celebrate with ice cream!" Kelsey suggested.

I laughed and hugged everyone close.

Even though the Falcons had won, even though Annie thought I had soccer scholarship potential, even though Jodie and I had made up and I wasn't self-conscious about my body anymore, the best thing about this week by far was the fact that I was with my family, both loving and being loved by them.

Still Hungry?
Here's a taste of the eighth book in the

series, **Donut Delivery**

Chapter 1
Freedom Week!

It's almost spring break at Bellgrove Middle School. The flowers are starting to bloom, the birds are showing off their springtime symphonies, and the whole town is smiling and enjoying spending time outdoors again.

This is when long pants start to fade away, sweaters go on vacay, and school hallways are suddenly sprinkled with tank tops, skirts, and shorts.

Normally, these early days of spring would be my

favorite time of year, but this year I was feeling a little annoyed by the change in weather.

I think it has to do with the fact that I'm in middle school now. Is it wrong for me to want to feel a little more grown-up in my clothes, and in my overall appearance?

And spring time at Bellgrove Middle School is also when it becomes abundantly clear to everyone who is allowed to shave their legs, and who isn't.

Can you guess which side of that fence I'm stuck on?

My mom is the assistant principal of my school, and let's just say that despite her chic, stylish, and modern clothes, she has some unfair ideas on stuff.

How she got the idea that her daughters shouldn't start shaving their legs until they're in high school is so unfair!

When I asked her why I have to wait until I'm in high school, what she told me was pretty simple. My mom's mom, grandma Rita, didn't let her daughters shave their legs until they were in high school.

That's it. That's the only reason. Leave it to my mom to carry on tradition, I guess. . . .

As for my dad, he's pretty protective of me and

my older sister and isn't exactly enthused about us looking too grown-up in any way, so he definitely had Mom's back on this one, like always.

"Mom, who cares if I have hair on my legs or not?" I tried to reason with her once.

Mom looked at me and smiled, like a cat who has just caught its evening meal.

"Exactly my point," she said. "So why go through all the trouble if no one cares . . . who are you trying to impress anyway, Casey?" she asked.

"No one!" I said.

But that wasn't 100 percent true, was it?

Mom got me thinking. I've had hair on my legs for some time now.

Why did I want to shave all of a sudden? Was it because the other girls my age were doing it? Or did I want to shave my legs for another reason?

My older sister Gabby, who's now a high school junior went through the same thing with this rule all through middle school. By the time she got to high school, she was one of the last girls in her class with unshaved legs.

Lucky for her, Gabby refused to wait.

I love how Gabby tells the story about the

morning she gracefully rebelled. She and Mom were out grocery shopping for family Sunday brunch.

This was a few years ago, right before Gabby was going to enter high school. They were doing self-checkout, the ones where you scan your own groceries.

Check this out. Right in front of our mom's face, Gabby took a packet of disposable razors and scanned it and put it in the bag, watching Mom the entire time she did it. The way she tells it, Mom gave her this strange look she'd never seen before, or since, and never said another word about it.

Gabby's had beautifully smooth legs ever since.

But that's my sister Gabby for you. Being a straight A student and the prima ballerina of Bellgrove High School, means she can sometimes color outside the lines and knows she'll get away with it.

Being an average student and all, I just don't see myself getting away with half the things Gabby does. I couldn't see myself being bold enough to do what Gabby did. Mom would be all over me if I even glanced at a pack of razors.

Speaking of my BFF, what I look forward to the most about spring break was getting to spend the whole week with Lindsay. We always plan out every day of our spring breaks down to the last second.

It's the one week we feel like we are free to do what we want, when we want. That's how we came to call spring break our "Freedom Week." Since we were little kids, we've spent as many of our spring breaks together as we possibly could. We've even had our parents agree to a few sleepovers during Freedom Week.

Actually, this has been going on since we were babies because of our moms. Back then, our moms planned our spring breaks since they both worked at the school and had off at the same time. Then, the four of us would spend almost all our spring breaks together, every year. We would watch movies, do projects, and later, go on hikes. Fun times!

As soon as we got to decision-making age, whenever that was, our moms left it up to us to plan our spring breaks.

So that's the long and short of how Freedom Week was born. Usually during Freedom Week we kept up the tradition of doing fun art projects and geeking out on our favorite movies.

But this year, now that we're in middle school, I

want to level up and do different stuff! For instance, I want to incorporate some acting exercises that we did in camp last summer.

I couldn't wait to tell Lindsay about my ideas for Freedom Week.

Just then I walked into the school lunchroom and headed straight for our usual table in the center, close to where the girls' soccer and field hockey teams sit.

Lindsay is no athlete and neither am I. She is a no-nonsense working girl and I'm an artist.

We don't really fit in to one particular group, so our nearby table is a hodgepodge of girls with some different and overlapping interests.

Our friend Michelle is a photographer, Lindsay's new friend Maria has a family that opened a cool Puerto Rican bakery in town, and Kelsey is Lindsay's friendly cousin on the field hockey team.

Overall lunch was a pretty cool scene.

Today Lindsay was the first one at our lunch table.

Perfect timing! I like when we can grab some moments alone before the other girls swoop in with their raucous laughter and hilarious dramas!

"Hey, tuna on rye," I said, sitting down.

"What's up, leftover lasagna," she answered back.

Lindsay had tuna on rye and I had, well, leftover lasagna. We smiled knowingly at each other because it was a comfort to know someone and be known so well. We always knew what the other was having based on the day of the week.

I noticed Lindsay was jotting something on a piece of paper nearby. When she finished, she raised her green catlike eyes to me and smiled.

"I've been brainstorming a list of movies that we can watch this week," she said.

"About Freedom Week," I said. "I was thinking we could watch movies along a certain theme. What do you think of anime?"

Lindsay's eyes slid back down to her paper.

"I have a couple animes on here but not a week's worth. Maybe we can have an anime day. Oh how about this? Each day we have a different movie theme? We can even have a scary movie night!"

"Great idea, Linds," I said. "I don't know when I became such an anime fan anyhow."

"Yeah, what's up with that?" Lindsay asked.

When I didn't say anything right away, Lindsay filled in the blanks. "Let me guess . . . Matt Machado?" she asked in a syrupy, singsong voice.

It took me a while to admit it, but Matt Machado is legit my first crush. I had met him at sleepaway camp that past summer, and we became the best of friends.

We're not old enough to be anything more than that, but if we were allowed to date, I wondered if we would be something more. I wasn't exactly sure how Matt or even I felt about that.

"Okay, Matt loves anime and now I'm hooked," I admitted, holding my head in my hands and groaning. Lindsay giggled.

"Hooked on anime . . . or Matt?" she asked.

I blushed and Lindsay waved it off.

"You're hopeless. Anyhow, let me know which animes you want to watch this week to add to the list."

"You're the best, Linds," I told her. "I can't wait for our glorious week of freedom."

"Same here. It's my favorite time of year because of you," Lindsay said. "I also love how we're carrying on something that our moms started."

A moment of silence followed. I knew it was because we were both thinking about Lindsay's mom, who has joined the angels.

I also thought about how much our friendship could use this quality time. Middle school has been hard on our friendship, especially since I came back from camp all boy crazy and artsy—two sides of me Lindsay had never seen before.

It put us in a sort of funky space for a while, but we'd worked through things. Still, we didn't exactly have the same level of comfort that we had before, and I was hoping that freedom week would help us to get it back.

I was also looking forward to taking my mind off Matt. He lives 10 hours away in a town called Hardwick.

I thought of him constantly . . . the memories we shared at camp, his handsome face burned into my mind, all the laughter we shared. From what Matt's mom told me (I met her a few times on the phone), Matt sounded pretty into me, too. She said they talk about me all the time.

As I rattled off some anime titles for Lindsay to write down, I gazed at my oldest friend in the world. Lindsay knew almost everything about me. Almost.

While she wrote, I admired the river of reddish brown hair flowing down her shoulders.

When I say Lindsay's my oldest friend, that's real talk. We were born a day apart and first met in the hospital nursery. Our moms were work friends before we came along, but having babies at the same time formed a bond between them that has outlasted Amy Cooper's death.

My mom says she can still feel her gentle, loving presence in the hallways at school. Somehow, my mom still feels really connected to Lindsay's mom even though she's no longer here.

Something that Lindsay and I used to have in common was our take on boys.

After all, Bellgrove boys have been grossing us out on the regular since kindergarten. Our vibe was to hate their guts until further notice.

Then I experienced something different at camp when I met Matt. He was different than any other boy I'd ever met.

First of all, he looked and smelled really good. Also, he wasn't some undercover or outright video game addict.

Instead, he has this black notebook that he takes with him everywhere because he's always writing stuff down that he sees, thinks and experiences. He's really interested in a bunch of stuff, and all the adults at camp adored him because he could talk about anything.

He looks up stuff he wants to learn about and doesn't try to act dumb or tough to fit in like other boys.

Matt's also in touch with his feelings. I remember him getting pretty emotional when he talked about when his mom married his stepdad years back. That's when his last name legally changed to Machado.

Also, Matt's biracial, just like me. This is something we had in common at camp which drew us closer together right away.

His biological dad, who left when Matt was a baby, was white, and his mom is black from the Caribbean. My parents, however, are the reverse: my dad's black and my mom's white.

Besides my sister, Matt's the only person who I know totally gets me for me.

The lunch room was beginning to fill up. I knew we wouldn't be alone at this table for much longer. Lindsay had to raise her voice in order for me to hear her.

"Matt sounds like a pretty cool guy, I'd love to meet him someday," she said.

"Yessss! That would be fire! We should call him on video chat sometime," I said, excited at the thought.

I wanted Lindsay to understand just what I saw in Matt, and I wanted Matt to put a face and a voice to the BFF I so often spoke about back at camp.

"Cool!" Lindsay agreed.

Even though I'm just about the only thing Lindsay and Matt have in common, I pictured them totally hitting it off.

Lindsay loves meeting new people. Unlike me, Lindsay's the type of small town girl that wants to someday leave Bellgrove for big city life and melt into the crowd and make a name for herself doing some awesome and unpredictable things.

It took Lindsay a little while to adjust to my changes.

Even though she accepts Matt's place in my life, I still catch her giving me these looks when I do certain things or when I bring him up a lot. Like when my phone lights up with a text message, and I snatch it up like it's my favorite candy bar that suddenly appeared out of thin air.

I never used to do that before this summer so it was pretty obvious to Lindsay that it had to do with Matt.

I guess to her I must look pretty obsessed. It was also kind of embarrassing because Matt hardly texts me anyhow. At first I thought it was because he had lost interest in me, but that turned out to be some fiction I created in my mind.

After weeks of not knowing what was up with this boy and his late one-word responses to all my texts I finally caught up with him one night and we texted for a good while.

That's when I found out that he was thinking about me every day too. He was just super busy and was always getting his phone taken away by his mom for disciplinary reasons. So it wasn't what I had thought at all!

After we had texted to clear the air, we started talking more on video chat. One Sunday morning, Matt and his family called during our Sunday brunch. It was fun but super awkward at points. Matt's mom and mine got along so famously that they ended up exchanging numbers soon after.

Now that Matt and I had come to a better understanding, and I was reminded by his amazingness, I began to miss my friend more than I did in the first place.

I guess that's when he officially became my crush.

The rest of our friends showed up to our table, so it was too late to spill my guts to Lindsay.

I was hooked on Matt more than I wanted to be, and I needed some advice on how to cure myself of this boy disease. It was no use bringing this stuff up to any of my friends who all saw boys as annoying creatures.

My sister was the only one who would really understand.

Even though I try not to run to Gabby for every single thing; she's basically my personal guru about life matters, and she always teaches me so much.

I haven't gone to her in a while about anything and this conversation was long overdue. I made it a point to go see her when I came home from school.

I couldn't wait until the school day was over.

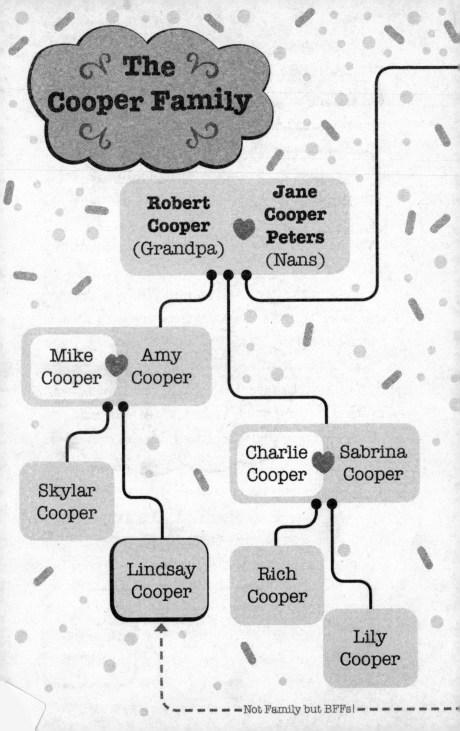

The Cooper Family

Robert Cooper (Grandpa) 💜 Jane Cooper Peters (Nans)

Mike Cooper 💜 Amy Cooper

Charlie Cooper 💜 Sabrina Cooper

Skylar Cooper

Lindsay Cooper

Rich Cooper

Lily Cooper

— Not Family but BFFs! —

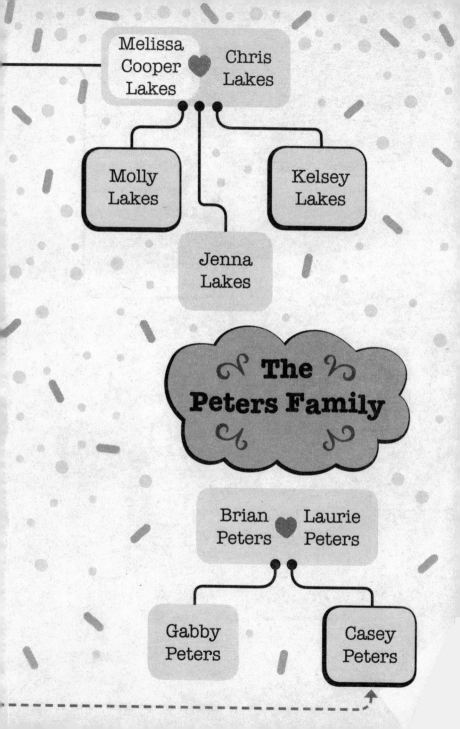

Melissa Cooper Lakes ♥ Chris Lakes

Molly Lakes

Kelsey Lakes

Jenna Lakes

The Peters Family

Brian Peters ♥ Laurie Peters

Gabby Peters

Casey Peters